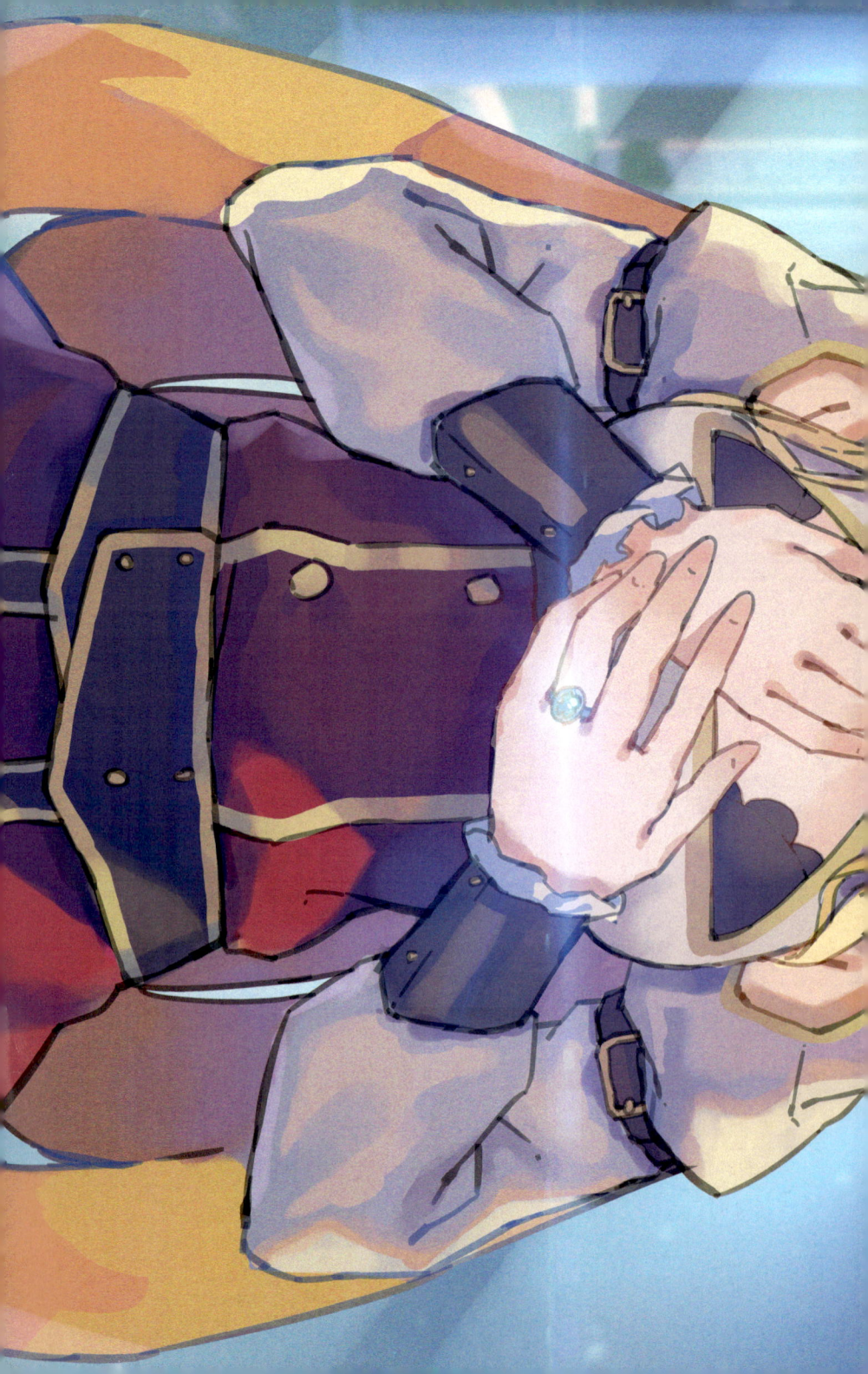

CONTENTS

Prologue An Old Story
001

Chapter 1 The Supporting Cast's Stories
003

Chapter 2 Dungeon Crawl
053

Chapter 3 Please Believe in My Love
097

Chapter 4 The End of an Adventure and a Day Off
127

Epilogue The Ring to Mark a Happy Ending
149

Afterword
181

Illustration: Yasumo
Design Work: Shindousha

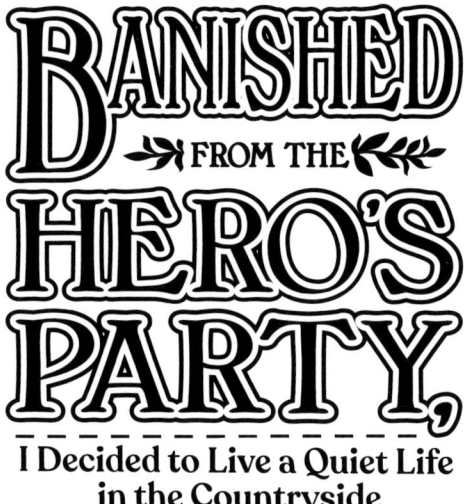

10

ZAPPON

Illustration by **Yasumo**

New York

Banished from the Hero's Party, I Decided to Live a Quiet Life in the Countryside, Vol. 10
Zappon

Translation by Dale DeLucia
Cover art by Yasumo

▼▼▼▼▼▼▼▼▼▼▼▼▼▼▼▼▼

This book is a work of fiction. Names, characters, places, and incidents are the product of the author's imagination or are used fictitiously. Any resemblance to actual events, locales, or persons, living or dead, is coincidental.

SHIN NO NAKAMA JYANAI TO YUUSHA NO PARTY WO OIDASARETANODE, HENKYOU DE SLOW— LIFE SURUKOTO NI SHIMASHITA Vol. 10
©Zappon, Yasumo 2022
First published in Japan in 2022 by KADOKAWA CORPORATION, Tokyo.
English translation rights arranged with KADOKAWA CORPORATION, Tokyo through TUTTLE-MORI AGENCY, INC., Tokyo.

English translation © 2024 by Yen Press, LLC

Yen Press, LLC supports the right to free expression and the value of copyright. The purpose of copyright is to encourage writers and artists to produce the creative works that enrich our culture.

The scanning, uploading, and distribution of this book without permission is a theft of the author's intellectual property. If you would like permission to use material from the book (other than for review purposes), please contact the publisher. Thank you for your support of the author's rights.

Yen On
150 West 30th Street, 19th Floor
New York, NY 10001

Visit us at yenpress.com
facebook.com/yenpress
twitter.com/yenpress
yenpress.tumblr.com
instagram.com/yenpress

First Yen On Edition: January 2024
Edited by Yen On Editorial: Jordan Blanco
Designed by Yen Press Design: Andy Swist

Yen On is an imprint of Yen Press, LLC.
The Yen On name and logo are trademarks of Yen Press, LLC.

The publisher is not responsible for websites (or their content) that are not owned by the publisher.

▼▼▼▼▼▼▼▼▼▼▼▼▼▼▼▼▼

Library of Congress Cataloging-in-Publication Data
Names: Zappon, author. | Yasumo, illustrator. | DeLucia, Dale, translator.
Title: Banished from the hero's party, I decided to live a quiet life in the countryside / Zappon ; illustration by Yasumo ; translation by Dale DeLucia ; cover art by Yasumo.
Other titles: Shin no nakama ja nai to yuusha no party wo oidasareta node, henkyou de slow life suru koto ni shimashita. English
Description: First Yen On edition. | New York : Yen On, 2020.
Identifiers: LCCN 2020026847 | ISBN 9781975312459 (v. 1 ; trade paperback) | ISBN 9781975312473 (v. 2 ; trade paperback) | ISBN 9781975312497 (v. 3 ; trade paperback) | ISBN 9781975312510 (v. 4 ; trade paperback) | ISBN 9781975333423 (v. 5 ; trade paperback) | ISBN 9781975343248 (v. 6 ; trade paperback) | ISBN 9781975343262 (v. 7 ; trade paperback) | ISBN 9781975343286 (v. 8 ; trade paperback) | ISBN 9781975350536 (v. 9 ; trade paperback) | ISBN 9781975367640 (v. 10 ; trade paperback)
Subjects: CYAC: Ability—Fiction. | Fantasy.
Classification: LCC PZ7.1.Z37 Ban 2020 | DDC [Fic]—dc23
LC record available at https://lccn.loc.gov/2020026847

ISBNs: 978-1-9753-6764-0 (paperback)
978-1-9753-6765-7 (ebook)

1 3 5 7 9 10 8 6 4 2
LBK

Printed in the United States of America

CHARACTERS

Red
(Gideon Ragnason)

Kicked out of the Hero's party, he headed to the frontier to live a slow life. Although not as powerful as Ruti, he's one of humanity's greatest swordsmen, with many feats to his name.

Rit
(Rizlet of Loggervia)

The princess of the Duchy of Loggervia and a former adventurer hailed as a hero. Now she is a truly happy young woman who has grown out of her combative phase and lives with the man she loves.

Ruti Ragnason

Red's younger sister and possessor of the Divine Blessing of the Hero, humanity's strongest blessing. Free at last from her blessing's impulses, she now enjoys life in Zoltan as a medicinal herb farmer while adventuring on the side.

Tisse Garland

A young girl with the Divine Blessing of the Assassin. An elite from the Assassins Guild, she is taking a break from her usual job and working with Ruti to get their medicinal herb farm running.

Yarandrala

A high elf Singer of the Trees capable of controlling plants. Brimming with endless curiosity, she has been through countless adventures during her long life.

Danan LeBeau

Humanity's strongest Martial Artist. He's overjoyed that he's finally done recovering. A natural musclehead who doesn't understand the concept of a slow life.

Van of Flamberge

A second Hero. Prince of a country destroyed by the demon lord's army. He's started to think about the purpose of the Divine Blessing of the Hero thanks to Red and the others.

Escarlata Dias (Esta)

Theodora hiding her identity. Hired to support Van the Hero because of her strength and experience. A masked warrior stunned by her abrupt, late-blooming first love.

Lavender

A small fairy. She met Van in a secret grove, fell in love with him, and pushed her way into the party. She is free-spirited and does not care about people. Van alone is special to her.

Prologue
An Old Story

Long ago, long before the Ancient Hero defeated the ancient demon lord and the era of humans rose from the ashes of the demon lord's empire, humans were nothing more than just one among a handful of species.

The name *Zoltan* did not yet exist. The wood elves who called this region home referred to the river that cut across the land as many things.

In the morning, it was called the river that reflected the sun rising over the great mountains.

Around noon, it became the white river where fish leaped from the surface.

Come evening, it was referred to as the time of rustling insect wings.

Then at night, it was dubbed the two dancing moons.

Wood elves believed that everything experienced constant change, and so they avoided giving things fixed names, instead trying to express the world in poetic phrases and metaphors. In their eyes, the scenes of today were a different world from the scenes of tomorrow.

However, there was an exception. This land known now as Zoltan had only a single wood elf name.

The Hero's Calamity.

But that is an old story.

Chapter 1
The Supporting Cast's Stories

Red & Rit's Apothecary.

I did a little stretching to clear the grogginess, bathed in the morning rays.

It was just yesterday that we came back from the fairy village, that I fought Van the Hero. I was happy everyone made it back safe and that I could return to my routine.

Unfortunately, not everything made it back.

"My bronze sword is broken."

My damaged sword leaned against the wall next to the door to the house. It had cleaved clean in two during the fight with Van. The other bronze sword I lent to Van for the battle was so bent out of shape that it didn't fit in its sheath.

It hadn't been able to endure the Hero's abilities, owing to the force of his attacks.

"If it weren't a battle with bronze swords, I would have died. I started using bronze swords out of stubbornness, hoping to avoid mortal fights after Ares forced me out of the party. To think that would genuinely end up saving my life…"

This wasn't the first time, either. When I fought Ruti after her Hero blessing was unleashed by the Sacred Avenger, a bronze sword's frailty was what saved Ruti and me.

"I wanted a powerful sword while traveling, but now that I'm taking it easy, I recognize that there are more important qualities."

The way of the sword was truly deep.

"Maybe I can open a local sword school when I'm a bit older."

Rit leaned out from the window. "What are you talking about?"

We had already said our good mornings. Since we slept in the same bed, waking up at roughly the same time was pretty standard. Whoever woke up first was always careful to get out of bed without rousing the other. Yet we still got up almost one after the other.

This morning, we shared a smile at how groggy our greetings were.

It was a small thing, but it was the pleasant start to another nice day nonetheless.

"A local sword school… Maybe I should teach the shotel."

"Hoping it will catch on in Zoltan?"

"Shotels are great. Just one can handle any situation!"

"Longsword or saber. Those were the official options for our knights, so I don't really know much about using a shotel."

"The Red- and Rit-style academy, offering the bronze-sword course and the shotel course."

"Yeah, that would be a pretty out-there school."

I'd been to plenty of different cities and villages, but I'd never seen a sword school with a combination like that. To be fair, no place specifically instructed people on how to use bronze swords. Shotels weren't popular in many regions, either.

It caught on in Loggervia because the southern mercenaries the duchy hired during the goblin king invasion fifty years ago wielded them. The mercenaries were granted residency as a reward for their efforts during the fighting, and so they shared their combat style, strengthening Loggervia's army. As a result, Loggervia became the only northern country where the shotel was a popular weapon.

"Shotels have so many uses, though."

Rit couldn't understand why her favored weapon wasn't more popular across the continent.

Honestly, I couldn't recommend it as a standard weapon for knights...

"Mrgh."

Seeing my face, Rit puffed her cheeks up, and she grabbed her practice shotel and handed it to me.

"I'm teaching you how to use one. Think of this as a continuation of your morning stretches!"

"I did learn the basics while I was knight, you know."

"Did you train to use a shotel yourself?"

"No, it was just practice to know how to deal with one if I encountered it during a fight."

"That alone can't convey a shotel's appeal. You have to be taught by someone who really understands its marvels."

I took the weapon from Rit.

"All right. May I ask for an introduction filled with passion for the shotel?"

"Leave it to me! My special training imbued with love for you and shotels will absolutely convince you!" Rit's cheeks turned red.

So cute.

* * *

A shotel is a double-edged sword that curves into a half circle. By making use of that curve, a shotel can cut into an opponent around a shield or pull a mounted enemy from their saddle. But that shape hampers its reach compared with a straight blade, and its center of gravity is also different, making it harder to use.

"Any Loggervian sword master would tell you a swordsman who relies on reach is no true warrior. If you want longer reach, use a pike, not a sword. Skillfully using the sword you have is proof you're a true fighter," Rit argued passionately.

Big, long weapons were showy, but superior reach also placed the cutting edge farther away from your hands.

In the Kingdom of Avalonia's teaching, the part farther from the hand was easier to stop. Blocking the end of an opponent's blade with the part of the sword near the cross guard and then shifting to a counterattack was one of the ideal forms of defense.

Someone who'd mastered defensive techniques with a single knife could easily defeat an unskilled longsword wielder who relied on strength.

"To a shotel user, the lack of reach isn't a handicap. C'mon, Red, raise your sword!"

I took a stance with the shotel Rit had given me.

"Hmmm, not quite." Rit moved behind me and reached around my body to adjust my stance. "Your right hand should be a little higher—raise your wrist… Yeah, more like that."

She physically adjusted me to fit what she envisioned.

"I'm pretty sure I was copying your stance," I said.

"My stance is an adaptation. *This* is more fundamental. Remember, this is what I taught Al before."

Al, huh? Kind of nostalgic. I hadn't seen him around in a while, but apparently, he was a full-fledged adventurer these days. Some people had even taken to calling him "the young genius of the blade." He probably wouldn't visit Zoltan much anymore.

"I'm sure he'll be glad to have the familiar sight of our shop when he does stop by."

"Yeah. We might not have many amazing medicines that are useful on a quest, but no one forgets their first adventure and starting equipment."

"Quaint items are part of an apothecary's charms."

We had a little laugh at that.

I practiced swinging a shotel with Rit, building up a bit of a sweat.

✻ ✻ ✻

"I'm done filling out the displays!"

"I finished checking the medicines that were ordered!"

We hurriedly went through the opening preparations.

Training with Rit proved so much fun that we lost track of time.

At this rate, we'd have to delay opening the store by ten minutes.

"Well, that's just the Zoltan way!"

"If anyone comes on the dot, we can give them some tea and ask them to wait a few minutes."

People in the capital would have found that infuriating.

In Zoltan, everyone was surprisingly indifferent to waiting or making other people wait.

During the old days, I would have grown annoyed thinking of all the things I could have done had I not been delayed.

We had so much to do back then—turning the tide on a world-scale war with just a handful of people. A journey to forcibly do the impossible with the power of the Hero. Massive battle lines that spanned the entire continent. Countries everywhere retreating and losing ground.

There was no just slipping off alone into dungeons to slay an evil mage or dragon for a quick and easy happily ever after.

The demon lord's army was a military organization with a well-developed hierarchy. If it lost a commander, another officer immediately assumed the position. That's not to say there was no disruption, but it wasn't enough to make their forces crumble. Our little party had to do the work of an army fighting the demon lord's troops. We needed to build a mountain from thousands of corpses with just a few people, and only then would we achieve a single victory. Once finished, it was time to do it again, over and over all around the continent, pushing the battle lines forward everywhere.

Even if that was God's role for the Hero, it was too unrealistic, if you asked me. So I'd tried to create situations where the human armies could win for themselves instead.

While my comrades had rested, I used my Lightning Speed to run to neighboring towns to gather information, negotiate with the local generals, and devise a strategy.

I'd decided what locations should be held and which ought to be abandoned. I hadn't been able to discuss it with Ruti because the Hero didn't allow her to ignore anyone in trouble.

That's why I had to be the one to do it.

"Red." Rit put her hand on my cheek. The warmth pulled me back to reality. "Let's have fun today!"

"Yeah, let's."

Those hard days were behind us.

The constant fighting had left something of a psychic scar, but my time spent here with Rit and Ruti, now free of her blessing, had saved me.

Only half a year ago, I couldn't sleep without a sword close by in case of an emergency. Knowing my weapon was broken would have kept me up all night.

Someone rang the doorbell.

"Welcome!" I greeted. "Sorry, we're still preparing to open. If you aren't in a rush, we'll provide some tea while you wait."

The old half-dwarf lady smiled gently. "That's no problem at all. I would love to have some tea."

After ten, the morning traffic calmed a bit.

The locals who'd kept inside all winter were venturing out more often as the days grew warmer. Admittedly, they'd all retreat back to their homes to escape the summer heat, but that was Zoltan for you.

This was the season when folk were most active and lively.

"The weather is great today!" Rit peered out the window.

The sky was bright and clear, a perfect spring day.

Spring was short-lived in this corner of the world. How many lovely days would we get this year?

That thought made today feel all the more special, so I took a spot next to Rit and looked out at the sky.

A breeze caressed my face.

This world was filled with fighting, but there were also tranquil moments, like standing with someone special and gazing outside.

Quiet times like this made me happier than any praise I ever received as a knight or a hero.

What did being a hero even mean? I worked to grow strong to protect Ruti. I never sought out the glory of heroism.

"Did you develop your skills in search of honor and glory?" I asked Rit.

"Hmmm."

She enjoyed the pleasant breeze as she thought on the question, likely recalling the days before we met.

"*Honor*'s probably not really the word for it. I just wanted to live my way."

"Your way?"

Rit was a princess of Loggervia.

The duchy was known as a major military power. Excluding its ally, the Kingdom of Avalonia, Loggervia had a few diplomatic problems with its neighbors. Possibly as a result, the aristocrats of Loggervia tended to hail from military lineages.

For all the battle in the nobility's blood, a princess like Rit, who'd run away from the castle to adventure in disguise, was a rarity.

"I wasn't the only one who snuck off, you know! Everyone talked about me being some improper princess, but when they were young, Father and my master traveled the world in disguise! A carefree princess who was never in line to inherit anything was nothing compared with Father—the crown prince—gallivanting around!"

"I see, so you got that from your dad, then?"

"He became a dignified ruler after taking the throne, marrying, and having children. He was wild in his youth, making it really weird that he tried to lecture me for sneaking off." Rit chuckled.

"But you love your father, right?"

"Mhm. A man who strove to be a dignified and coolheaded king for his country's sake, a father who cared for and watched over his family, and a swordsman who wished to run wild and free. Father was complex and contradictory, but I respect how he tried to be himself without giving up any portion of his identity."

I'd spoken with the duke briefly in the past, but I'd never seen anything more than the wise ruler who coolly analyzed the state of the war.

A leader capable of granting a party of outsiders command of Loggervia's best-trained fighting force was rare. Even a knight like me understood just how much courage that decision took.

Undoubtedly, it had been a painful choice, too. The duke was the sort of man capable of swallowing that bitter pill.

"Ha-ha, I'm not surprised he only ever showed you his stern side. However, the night he made that decision, Father broke his practice shotel during training," Rit said.

"Did he? I see…"

"The worry in his heart came out in his fighting. For a master like Father to snap his sword…"

Rit had competed with us when our party arrived in Loggervia.

Hoping to overturn the decision to relinquish command of the royal guard to the Hero's party, she'd tried to prove that Loggervia could protect itself alone. Her actions had partly been motivated by the fact that her master, Gaius, was commander of the royal guard, and she didn't wish to see him humiliated. Still, I imagine she was upset to see her father mortified over his inability to protect his nation, too.

"Okay, getting back to the question of why I ran away from the castle to go adventuring…" Rit looked at me. Standing at the window as we were, I felt the warmth of her body, and she mine. "…I didn't want to become a hero. I ended up being called one because of what I did, but it was never the goal."

"So why did you do it?"

"Freedom. I wanted to live my way, to do what I wished. I ran off to save someone. I fought because there were evil people I couldn't forgive. And when I wanted to be a princess, I came back and behaved like one. I tried to save Loggervia because I love it. It was always me living how I liked. Being a hero would have tied me down."

"Tied you down?"

"Right, that image of heroism. Brave and fearless, never crying, the ideal that everyone looks up to. I didn't want to be that sort of person. I preferred the freedom to run away to save my life if necessary, to cry, to get mad."

"I see. Beautiful. That's just like you."

"That's the reason I adventured. And it's the same now." Rit put her arms around my neck and hugged me. "I'm free, and I'm here because I want to be here. I want to be with you forever. That was true when I adventured, and it still is when I hug you blissfully. That will never change."

"You're strong."

Being with Rit had helped me stand again.

I wrapped my arms around her back and returned the embrace.

"Thanks, Rit."

"Heh-heh. Thank you, Red."

I was with her because it was what I wanted, too.

A feeling swelled inside me…

…and that's when the bell chimed again.

We immediately broke apart and reassumed typical business demeanor.

""Welcome!""

Although retired, we were still battle-hardened veterans.

Switching from an embrace to serious mode before the door opened was easy.

"So hard at work even on such a nice day? I'm impressed."

"Hello, Dr. Newman. If you have an order, I would have been happy to deliver it for you," I said.

"It's such a nice day that I felt like taking a little stroll."

I nodded. "I was just thinking of going for a walk with Rit later."

"That's a good idea. Ah, I'd like two dozen painkillers and the same number of hemostatics and bandages."

"That's quite a lot. Should I carry them to your clinic?"

"No, that's all right. When I was young, I worked as a traveling doctor and lugged around a box of medicine, so that won't be a problem."

Dr. Newman took the medicine I laid out on the counter for him and started packing it into his leather bag.

"...How is Cardinal Ljubo's condition?" I asked.

"The danger has passed. We got to him too late for healing magic to be much help, so he won't be able to move for a while, and the scars will remain, but he will survive. He has tremendous vitality, and his determination to survive is far beyond that of an average person."

"I guess it makes sense for someone who's climbed so high among the church ranks."

"He's not the sort you see here in Zoltan."

A shadow crossed Dr. Newman's face.

Ljubo was currently his patient. Apparently, Van had stabbed Ljubo after losing control. Such a terrible wound would have slain a normal adventurer on the spot. However, Ljubo possessed the powerful Divine Blessing of the Cardinal, and he was high enough of a level to travel with Van.

More than anything, he was fortunate to be injured at an inn, as he was quickly discovered and taken for treatment.

The only healer who could get to him quickly was a person with a low level that only afforded them weak healing spells. Fortunately, that sustained Ljubo long enough for Dr. Newman to arrive.

"...Are you all right?" I asked. "Ljubo ruined your teacher's life."

The doctor whom Newman had studied under had been wrongfully banished as a heretic by Ljubo at the behest of other medical professionals who'd bribed the cardinal.

"I cannot help but hate him, and I admit I've thought about killing him. The tiniest mistake on my part would have meant his death."

"It is rough having to save your enemy, but killing a powerful member of the church isn't something you can sweep under the rug. Even if it was a medical mistake, or perhaps *especially*, considering your blessing is the Doctor, they would blame you for not fulfilling your blessing's role and have an inquisitor take you away."

"It's pretty rough when a doctor's error is dubbed heresy. Naturally, I'm being careful not to make any mistakes."

"If a cardinal dies, the church will make it a huge deal and force the matter. So...maybe it would be better to entrust Ljubo to another clinic?"

Dr. Newman shook his head. "Red, I'm not that devout when it comes to the church's teaching. I had a pretty terrible experience with one of their inquisitors, after all. But I'm grateful to God for this."

"Grateful?"

"I spoke to Ljubo about everything. When he realized he couldn't move and that someone who hated him controlled whether he lived, his face froze in terror...and he begged for forgiveness."

"I'm sure. He's the sort who would lower his head to anyone to survive."

"But I didn't forgive him. I doubt I ever will."

A dark rage clouded Dr. Newman's usual warm expression.

"But you didn't kill him," I said.

"Of course not. I'm a doctor. No matter how much I might hate him, as a doctor, I must save his life. That's what I learned from my teacher. As the student of a doctor who lost his hands needlessly and still tried to leave behind his knowledge for me to save the sick, I settled things with Ljubo."

"Settled?"

"I'm trying to beat the past that's tormented me."

"I see. So that's why you have to be the one to heal him."

Dr. Newman smiled at that. After checking the medicine, he put the bag over his shoulder.

"Thank you. I was looking for someone to talk about this with," he said.

"If a simple apothecary like me will do, I'll lend an ear anytime. Especially for such a valuable client."

"Just a typical sort of conversation between a simple apothecary and a simple doctor."

After a smile, Dr. Newman returned to his clinic, and the shop was quiet.

"Everyone has their own burden to bear." Rit sounded moved.

All the people who came to our shop had their stories, just like we did. And they all came with baggage.

"Trouble like that is why I didn't want to make Ruti shoulder the fate of the world alone simply because she was the Hero."

Everyone lived their own story.

Should a fight between a girl who happened to be born with the Hero blessing and the demon lord who coincidentally possessed the Demon Lord blessing really decide everything?

Were others merely bit players in the grand story of the Hero and the demon lord?

"I can't accept that we're all so insignificant. Whatever Demis's will, the people's wants matter," I said.

Being born with the right blessing didn't matter. Anyone who tried to save the world of their own volition was a hero. Even without the tremendous strength of the Hero, if many good people worked together, they would save the world.

"Thinking back, I got in the way so much in Loggervia, but you were never harsh with me," Rit remarked.

"From a strategic perspective, it was a gigantic pain. Someone who acknowledged us as heroes and knew our strength yet still desired to save her homeland was a dazzling sight to behold."

"Ehehe."

"Also, it was cute how you charged forward, full of confidence, only to mess up."

"Ugh." Rit's expression stiffened, and her cheeks turned a little red.

In the old days, she was a little too focused on antagonizing us and didn't fully comprehend the might of the demon lord's army. The demon lord's forces wouldn't lose to someone that blind to their true enemy.

"Nearly half a year has passed since Ruti quit, yet the war situation isn't too bad," I remarked.

Rit nodded. "Supposedly, humanity is slowly starting to win."

Humans took repeated losses for a while, but Ruti the Hero's efforts bought time for the armies to regroup.

The strength of the demon lord's army was far superior to that of any nation on the continent, but it had to cross a great ocean. Plus, humanity had greater numbers.

Countries had refused to cooperate with one another, instead focusing on myriad smaller, short-term goals. This led to victories for the demon lord's army. Raising troops and crossing a border to aid a neighboring land was no simple feat. Did Demis think that humanity would unite around the Hero once the armies of evil attacked? Nations would refuse to cooperate even if the world was ending tomorrow. The possible balance of power the day after tomorrow too often claimed precedence.

Things had since changed, though. Veronia previously maintained a stance of neutrality while supporting the demon lord's army from the sidelines, but now it fought for humanity. Almost every nation on the continent was battling together as one.

Meanwhile, the demon lord's forces had lost a key to their invasion, the air supremacy of Gandor of the Wind and the wyvern knights. Similarly, Altra of the Water and the serpent divisions had been wiped out by Esta.

Losing a pair of leaders and their troops weakened the demon lord's army considerably. It was unable to hold the territory it had claimed and was slowly ceding it back to the nations of Avalon.

Yielding a bit of ground hardly meant the demon lord's army was out of the fight, but at the current rate, it was poised to be overwhelmed by humanity.

"The shrinking front line will prove advantageous for the enemy, though."

If the demon lord's troops relinquished some land and fell back to a more manageable position, they would have an easier time coordinating offensives. Humanity's counterattack would likely stall at the fortress along the border of the former Flamberge Kingdom.

Deadlocked battle lines were typically a call for negotiations and an armistice to end the conflict. Unfortunately, there was still no sign of any diplomacy from the demon lord's army. No one knew whether its leaders were open to the idea.

Even if humanity broke past the fortress thanks to the work of some brilliant strategist and then went on to eliminate all enemies on the continent, human shipbuilding and naval knowledge could not weather the seas around the dark continent. The demon lord's army would survive.

Attacking the demon lord's territories and wholly eradicating the menace was impossible.

"But that's something for kings and generals to worry about," I said.

Rit shrugged. "Right, it's not like we know what the demon lord's after."

"It feels wrong to dub the invaders an army of evil created by God, then never devote any greater consideration to it. The current demon lord must have a goal." Despite saying as much, I couldn't think of one.

In the past, I'd tried not to ponder the topic.

A story about discovering why the Hero and the demon lord existed instead of one about the Hero defeating the demon lord. It promised to be a grand quest that would challenge God and the world.

Back when I searched for a way to free Ruti from the Hero, I had researched her blessing.

Using my position as second in command of the Bahamut Knights of the Kingdom of Avalonia, the largest nation on the continent, I'd plumbed every record I could get my hands on.

Yet the answer always eluded me. To find anything more, I required access to the secret church archives at the Last Wall fortress.

Those records were open only to the father and cardinals. Undoubtedly, the history of the church that was the proxy for God contained something that could lead me closer to the purpose of the Hero and the demon lord.

There probably wouldn't be much more than some old story, though. That's what I assumed, anyhow.

"At the very least, I need to do what I can here for Van before he resumes his journey," I said.

As the Guide who once traveled with a different Hero, I had a responsibility to Van if he intended to fight and fulfill his role.

"When did you get the idea to return to the ancient elf ruins?" Rit asked.

"I guess after Van stabbed Cardinal Ljubo," I replied.

Rit grimaced. "That definitely made it clear how unstable he was."

"I never imagined his blessing might run wild like that. According to the church's teachings, such a thing shouldn't be possible for the Hero, so it's not surprising I never came across anything like it in the records."

The Hero lost sight of himself and attempted to kill his comrade.

What if this isn't the first time something like that has occurred?

"I'm going to check on Cardinal Ljubo tomorrow and then make plans," I said.

Rit nodded. "Then let's take it easy today, in case things start getting busy later."

"Sounds good. We can worry about tomorrow's problems tomorrow."

Rit beamed from her spot beside me.

I set all other thoughts aside to focus on spending time with her.

∗   ∗   ∗

"What do you think? About time to make lunch?" I asked.

"Yeah!"

I couldn't help but smile at the cheerful response.

Rit and I started living together last summer. Preparing lunch for her had become commonplace, but she was always delighted.

And because she was so clearly happy about it, I took great joy in it as well.

Nothing about today was exceptional, yet…

"All right, I'll put in a little extra effort to make something really delicious."

"Really?! What are you going to make?!"

"Hmm, how about spring vegetables with steak on the side?"

"Not the other way around?"

"No, the vegetables are the main dish, and the steak is the side."

"Fresh, seasonal vegetables are delicious. I can't wait!"

After an excited send-off from Rit, I headed to the kitchen.

Now to put all my knowledge to work and make some lunch.

I retrieved a basket of spring vegetables we'd received as payment for medicine.

"They all look nice and fresh. We should enjoy them while they're still tasty."

I smiled a little, and the scent of onion stoked my hunger.

The meat was nothing special, but these vegetables were top-class. They were perfect for a main course.

Peas, asparagus, and onion cooked in a paprika-butter glaze.

Mushrooms and baby broccoli in a garlic sauté, oven-baked anchovies with cheese and paprika, and simple vegetables grilled in olive oil.

And for meat, I used a beef roast I'd purchased for a stew. I carefully sliced the tendons to soften the roast before tenderizing it and prepared a tomato-based sauce that would pair well with all the greens.

It was well past noon by the time lunch was ready.

Each dish was simple, but there were too many for a household kitchen to handle… I'd gotten a bit carried away.

The white bread and a pitcher of water with cut lemon and herbs floating in it were the final pieces.

"Sorry to keep you waiting, Rit! Can you help me set this out on the table?!"

"I've been looking forward to this!"

The joy in her reply was palpable.

I hung a sign on the door saying we were away for lunch.

With two of us running the place, we could alternate breaks to keep from outright closing, but that logic stood no chance against the temptation to enjoy eating together.

"Thanks for the meal!" Rit said excitedly.

Steak juices seeped from the meat when I cut into it.

The buttery sweet and colorful vegetables glistened from the glaze, and the green colors of the garlic sauté were appropriately spring-like.

The red paprika and melted cheese atop the baked anchovies were delightful.

Although the grilled vegetables were only a casual assortment, the simplicity brought out a delicious freshness.

And to top it all off, the hint of lemon and herbs from the water in our cups proved refreshing.

Rit reached for the garlic sauté.

"Mmmm! That's good!" She broke into a smile. "The texture is great!"

Mushroom and baby broccoli possessed a crisp, crunchy texture. That was especially true when they were fresh.

Next, Rit took a bite of the meat.

"And it goes great with steak."

The beef was cooked to a slightly pink medium well, tender enough that a knife passed through it easily.

It wasn't expensive meat, but proper preparation had turned it into an easy-to-eat steak.

"Mm! Today's lunch is great!"

Rit's blissful reaction was the greatest reward possible.

I reached for the garlic sauté.

Eating with Rit made it even tastier than when I'd checked the flavor in the kitchen.

* * *

After lunch, we returned to work.

And after a little while.

"Riiit, I'm here!"

The voice was quiet, but it still carried clearly from the door.

"Lavender?" I said.

A little fairy entered the shop. "I hate you, Red! Bleh!" Lavender stuck out her tongue when she saw me.

"Not a fan, huh?"

"You're the human who hurt Van! I'll hate you until the end of time itself!"

Despite her words, she didn't attack me, and that was proof that we'd built up a good enough relationship.

Lavender was a particularly special being, even among fairies. Her true name was Ketu, the archfay of calamity. Her small form was a facade and seal that contained her true nature. She was a mythical creature capable of holding her own against Rit and Ruti together, and that was if she held back. At full strength, she likely surpassed the demon lord's four heavenly kings.

"If you had been around during our journey, the fighting would have been a lot easier," I remarked.

"I don't intend to travel with anyone other than Van! And I happen to like this form because Van said I'm cute. I won't do anything to break this form when I'm with Van!"

"So the other day was an exception, then?"

"Van was in trouble… I am a little grateful that you helped him. But that doesn't change the fact that you hurt him, so I hate you!"

Lavender glared at me.

I grimaced slightly and looked at Esta, who stood behind the fairy.

"No matter what anyone might say, I've come to believe that Lady Ruti's party was the more orthodox of the two." She grinned from behind her mask. "The present one consists of Van the incomplete hero, the calamitous and fickle fay Lavender, the greedy and worldly Cardinal Ljubo, a mysterious and masked wannabe guide, and Albert, who's running around taking care of things for me. Even our goals are scattered…"

"If I can be useful to everyone by running around, then I couldn't ask for more." Albert had arrived.

"I hate you, too!" Lavender stuck her tongue out at Esta and flew over to Rit. "Hey, Rit! Let's chat more about love! Esta's always talking about boring things!"

"After work," Rit replied.

"What if I go get a big gold nugget? That's worth more than the bits of silver you'll earn from running a place like this, right? If I put a little pressure on the fairies, they'll bring me one right away."

"How crude."

Lavender stuck her tongue out again at my remark.

Archfay were generally adored by others of their kind, often becoming leaders of fairy villages. I understood why others avoided Lavender, though. Admittedly, that was less about her being selfish and more because she was a being of calamity.

"I know you're thinking something mean about me," Lavender said, eyes narrowed.

"Not at all. I was just pondering fairies in general," I replied.

For all their intelligence, fay creatures were closer to monsters than people.

They were not beings to be humanized, yet it was very easy to imagine Lavender bullying weaker fairies the way a person would.

"I'm sure you could get quite a lot of gold relatively easily, Lavender," Rit said.

"Mhm, humans are so strange, desperately chasing after bits and pieces of gold and silver! They're so easy to gather!"

"But to me, the time I spend working with Red is worth more than any treasure."

Lavender looked like she suddenly had a revelation.

It was a bit embarrassing hearing that while standing next to them, but apparently, putting it so bluntly helped Lavender understand.

"If that's the case, then I guess there's no helping it. I'll have some wine while I wait in the back." Lavender flew off into the living room as though she owned the place.

Sheesh, fairies are troublesome.

But human logic meant nothing when it came to them. Shrugging and laughing it off was the best I could do.

"That's Lavender, I guess. Why did you come by, Esta?" I asked.

"Sorry for the trouble. I'd intended it to be just Albert and me, but when I said we were going to your shop, Lavender insisted on coming. Apologies for the disruption, but it *is* a good sign."

"It's fine," Rit answered. "I don't mind talking about love with Lavender. She doesn't understand human sensibilities, but she gets along well with those she likes."

"I see. Lavender has never had any affection for me, so I never knew that," Esta said.

I gave a weak smile. "Sounds like you've got a rough journey ahead."

"Isn't that the truth?" Esta mirrored my expression. "As for why I came..."

"Ah, if you wanted some tea, I could make some," I offered.

"Tea would be nice. It's not a pressing matter... I just wished to report on Van's condition and to speak about the upcoming adventure."

"I see. Rit told Lavender she'd have to wait until the workday was finished, but should we close up to talk now?" I said.

Esta chuckled a little. "No, I'll wait until evening, too. It's not such a priority that it has to get in the way of your time together."

She had really grown more flexible. It was surprising from the perspective of someone who'd known her for so long.

"In that case..." Rit seemed to hit upon an idea. A shallow smirk formed on her face, as though she'd thought up a trick. "There is a nice café a short walk from here. The coffee is delicious."

Esta considered it for a moment. "Coffee, huh? But a pointless stroll..."

"Since you came all the way to this part of town, it would be a waste not to try it. It's fine. Albert doesn't have anything to do, either, so the two of you can go."

"Together with Albert?!" Esta looked flustered.

I never knew she could turn so red...

Even I kept my cool when eating with Rit after we reunited...right?

A vague memory of Nao making fun of us for acting like a couple of teenagers flashed through my mind, but I decided to ignore that.

"Forcing Albert to walk that much would be improper," Esta said.

"Eh? Ah, not at all. It isn't that far. I've been there several times before," Albert replied.

"Right, you used to live here...but we came to discuss Van, so there's no cause to leave the apothecary," Esta reasoned.

Albert nodded. "That's true. Although, it is a bit of a shame. One of my old comrades, a woman named Ria, took me there once. Rit's right. The coffee is quite nice."

"What? You went with a woman?"

Esta's expression changed! Well, she was wearing a mask, so I couldn't really say what her face looked like, but she was shaken enough that it was evident despite the mask.

"What are you, a teenager?" I couldn't help myself. Rit laughed, and Albert just cocked his head in confusion.

"Yes, right after the Zoltan Adventurers Guild introduced me to Ria, we needed to build some connection and trust. I was still new to Zoltan, so she and my other party members invited to me to eat with them," Albert explained.

"I...see..." Esta sounded dejected.

She was a pure paladin who'd devoted herself to religion and combat from childhood. Esta had focused on her mission, training knights and mastering the spear without getting involved in the church's power struggles. She never desired to lead her own parish one day.

Esta was the sort who stoically went about her work, believing that was all there was to her life. A freer existence was a foreign concept, and on top of that, she was falling in love.

It was akin to a lifelong merchant picking up a sword for the first time. They overreacted to every one of the opponent's reactions. From an outside perspective, it was an incredibly strange way to brandish a weapon.

Being a spectator for once was pretty fun.

"I get the feeling you are thinking something rude about me," Esta said.

I shook my head. "No, not at all."

The masked woman narrowed her eyes at me. I chuckled and decided to throw her a lifeline.

"You always send Albert out on errands, right?"

"Mrgh, I just…"

"Rewarding an attendant for their hard work is part of a knight's duty, isn't it?"

"…Th-that's right, *ahem*." Esta nodded, then forced a little cough.

No, really, that was seriously forced.

"Mm, Albert."

"Yes, ma'am?"

"You always help me. As a knight, a trustworthy attendant is more valuable than any magic gear."

The circuitousness was killing me, and Rit fought back giggles desperately.

"It isn't much as a reward, but would you like to have coffee together?"

"Thank you very much. It really is an excellent café, so I would gladly take you there."

"Um. Mhm, p-please do…," Esta answered awkwardly.

Nothing like this would've happened while we were traveling together. This scene was only possible after Theodora became Esta.

I lacked any proof, but I had the feeling that she could become stronger as Esta than as Theodora.

Esta wouldn't struggle as much thinking about what she could offer when the Hero outpaced her in strength. At least, that's what I thought.

Albert turned from Esta to me. "Also, I have a request for you, sir."

"You do?"

There was a serious look on his face. I stood up from my chair.

"After today's meeting, I would like for you to spar with me."

Esta regarded Albert with surprise; however, her expression softened after a moment. "Please, Red. I would appreciate it, too."

✱   ✱   ✱

Albert and I cut an interesting contrast. We'd both been pushed out of a party for lacking strength. I was ousted because of the Guide's limits, and Albert was dropped because he couldn't manifest the Champion's potential.

The difference was that I gave up and searched for an easier, slower life for myself, while Albert never gave up on being a hero.

He'd taken one of the paths I could have.

Rit and I closed up shop for the evening. Lavender had finished helping herself to plenty of wine, and Esta and Albert were back from the café.

Albert and I stood across from each other in the backyard, holding wooden swords.

"We don't know how long the discussions will take, so I figured we ought to do this first, before it gets too dark," I said.

"Thank you very much, sir."

Albert's reply was refreshingly polite.

He's become such a nice young man.

"So can he win?" Lavender sipped from her small cup of wine. Apparently, she intended to spectate.

"It would be pretty difficult for the Albert I knew. What do you think, Esta?" Rit said.

Esta shook her head. "Of course not. He has absolutely no chance of winning."

"What? Fighting even if he can't win? Humans really enjoy meaningless things."

"The meaning is in the battle, not the victory. Being a swordsman is a far deeper thing than you think," Esta replied.

Lavender shrugged. "Doesn't make any sense to me."

Esta kept her eyes fixed on Albert.

"May I begin?" Albert asked.

"Yeah, come at me however you like. Or would you rather I start it?" I replied.

"No, sir."

Albert raised the sword in his left hand.

He'd lost his right during a battle with me. He'd since acquired a prosthetic to help, but it couldn't manage the delicate and forceful movements necessary to wield a sword.

The two-handed, heavy weapons Albert once brandished were beyond him now.

"I'll start." Albert disappeared. "Martial Art: Swallow's Approach!"

The technique closed the distance to the target quickly for a swift attack. It was popular among swordsmen with high blessing levels. When fighting monsters, it was quite useful, but…

"Gfh!"

My wooden sword sank into Albert's stomach, causing him to buckle.

"Red?!" Rit shouted.

Lavender looked surprised. "Whoa, that Red guy's merciless, hitting that hard."

I didn't let it bother me, though, and took a step back from Albert, who writhed on the ground.

"Swallow's Approach can only move in a direct line toward your opponent, and the distance of the leap forward is fixed. An opponent familiar with it can easily read its travel."

"Hah, hah… So that's how you deflected my magic blade so easily the last time." Albert took a few moments to catch his breath and stand back up. "Gh!"

This time, he took a big step forward with his left leg, thrusting without a Martial Art.

I stepped back with my right leg, evading while also hitting Albert's shoulder.

"Ugh…"

Albert slumped and clutched the spot I'd struck.

Wooden sword or not, that had been a serious attack. An ordinary fighter would've been down and out.

"That looks painful... Does he hate Albert?" Lavender asked.

Rit looked a bit stunned, too.

"Albert!" Esta shouted. "I'll heal you no matter your injuries! Fight until you're satisfied!"

"Thank you...Lady Esta!"

I waited for Albert to stand back up.

Upon seeing that he could move again, I went on the attack.

I neutralized his counterattempt and beat him to the ground a third time.

And from there, the fighting continued until Albert couldn't stand.

※　　　　　※　　　　　※

"Here, you must be thirsty, right?"

"Thank you very much. I appreciate it."

Albert took the cup I offered.

Esta's healing magic had mended his wounds, but spells couldn't restore lost stamina.

After getting that battered, it wouldn't be surprising for Albert to be out for the night. That he managed to keep sitting was impressive.

Esta and the others had gone back inside, but Albert and I were taking a short break outside before joining them.

"Did you get what you wanted?" I asked.

"Yes, sir. I feel much better having you fight me seriously. Last time, I lost without understanding what happened."

When we clashed before, I defeated him as he swung his sword around furiously.

"I knew I wouldn't win a rematch, but I wanted it to be a proper duel to learn how and why I failed. I hoped to understand the sword that changed my life."

"Sorry about your hand."

"It was a fight to the death. Sparing my life was mercy enough. And there are many things I've learned since losing that hand." Albert rubbed his prosthetic. "My blessing level has risen significantly, and I think I've gotten stronger. But as a swordsman, it has been limiting."

"Danan's the only person who could lose their dominant hand and somehow end up stronger for it."

Albert's sword was bereft of liveliness. His thrusts were swift, yet they lacked precision and impact.

Switching to a one-handed style after fighting two-handed demanded new maneuvers he'd never considered before. It wasn't an easy switch.

"Esta's teaching you, right?"

"You can tell?"

"Well, she's the only one in that party who could instruct someone in practical one-handed swordsmanship. It wasn't too hard to deduce."

"Ha-ha. For everyone else in the party, traditional combat techniques are secondary at best."

"Yeah."

We shared a laugh over Esta's struggles.

"I am weak," Albert declared.

"That's not true at all. As you are now, you could proudly make it as a B-rank adventurer at the guild in Central. With the right party members, you might even reach A-rank."

"But I'm not strong enough to survive the battles of the Hero's journey, right? Because I'm a bad match for my blessing."

"..."

"I will most likely die somewhere along the way." Albert seemed at peace as he said that.

"You'll fight to ensure you live, won't you?" I asked.

"Of course. But I am still ready for what happens."

I was unsure what to say.

I wanted to tell him that if he intended to die before even starting, it was better to quit this route. But did I really have the right to deny his resolution?

"That's why I wanted to know your true sword before I left Zoltan. This might well be my last chance to meet with you or see Zoltan again." Albert stood, wobbling a bit. "It was an enjoyable fight. Thank you, sir."

"...Wait a moment."

I hurried inside and came back with a bundle I'd tucked away in the back of the storage room.

"I want to lend you this."

"What is it?"

Albert undid the wrapping, revealing a broken longsword.

"This is my trusty blade. The one I found during my journey."

"Your sword!"

"Its name is Thunderwaker. We found it in an old lord's tomb. It wound up like this after taking an attack from Ruti the Hero."

"A sword that stopped a blow from the Hero."

"It's broken, but if you take the upper part of the blade and take it to a master smith, it should be the right length for a shortsword that can be wielded one-handed."

"Break a hero's blade?!"

"So that the next hero can use it. I'm sure that's what Thunderwaker wants."

Albert looked troubled, unsure if he was worthy of this. His strength was yet incomplete. And he'd been arrested as a criminal in Zoltan. He was uncertain whether he could be called a hero.

"I think of you as a hero," I said. "I told you as much the last time we fought."

"You told me I have the determination a hero needs...and I still find myself doubting that."

"I never would have been able to risk my life to stop Van when he went on his rampage."

"Huh? But that's exactly what you did."

"Only because I created a situation where I could win. I wouldn't have done the same in your position."

"...But I was just desperately stalling for time. Had Lady Esta not come, I would've died pointlessly."

I shook my head. "But you won. You beat an opponent who was overwhelmingly superior because of the strength of your resolve. I can't match that."

The Guide didn't have a skill that could bring about a miracle. If I knew I couldn't win, I would retreat. That was my limit.

"You are worthy of this sword. Please, Thunderwaker."

"I understand..." Albert rewrapped the broken sword. "Thank you, sir. I will fight well, so as not to dishonor this weapon."

"I didn't give it to you so you'd get all worked up," I said with a smile. "This sword saved my life when I had my back against the wall with no way out. I believe it will do the same for you. When everything is done, come back to Zoltan and tell me all about the battles you went through with this blade."

"So you're telling me to come back alive."

"That's right. Come back alive."

I wasn't going to speak some blatant lie like "I'm sure you'll survive." Saving the world was a deadly task. Still, I'd hope for his safe return. I wanted to see Esta and Albert living in peace and happiness together at the end of their journey.

I wanted their story to have a happy ending.

"Understood... I will come to see you again."

"I'm looking forward to it."

I meant that from the bottom of my heart.

* * *

Come night, Rit, Esta, Albert, Lavender, and I all gathered in the living room.

"Are you all right now?" Esta asked Albert.

"Yes, ma'am, I have rested enough. Sorry to keep you waiting."

"Don't worry about it... Also, you've got a good look on your face now." Esta smiled happily at Albert.

"You think so?" he said.

Esta turned to me. "Thank you, Red."

"Glad I could help."

With that, we moved to the main topic.

"Okay, how is Van faring, Esta?" I asked.

"It's safe to say he is stable now. The Hero blessing and his religious self-righteousness have both eased significantly. He is in much better condition now."

"Good. Sounds like he's well enough for me to check on him."

I'd meet with him and Ljubo tomorrow.

"Is the *Vendidad* ready to leave port?"

Esta nodded. "Yes, it's ready to go at any time...though it would be best to put together a new crew once we reach the next large town. Morale is too low from Van's leadership."

"Sounds rough, but not something to worry about while you're in Zoltan."

Van had thought it was a good and happy thing for people to die for the sake of the Hero's quest. From a religious perspective, that wasn't too strange, but to the sailors being treated as disposable tools, it probably felt a little too harsh.

There was no way they'd trust Van again. Deserters were bound to pop up in the coming months.

"So you can leave right after we've finished exploring the ruins and Cardinal Ljubo recovers," I said.

"Depending on the situation, we might also leave Ljubo here and return to the front lines sooner," Esta replied.

"Huh? You'd abandon him in Zoltan?" I didn't mask my distaste. Lavender burst into laughter, gripping her stomach. "What a cold fairy, laughing when one of your comrades almost died."

"I don't want to hear that from the person who looks so upset about a half-dead man remaining in town," she snapped back.

Lavender had a point, but Ljubo's prolonged presence in Zoltan was bound to cause some kind of issue.

"If he can move, we will take him with us. He doesn't want to be separated from the Hero anyway," Esta asserted.

Cardinal Ljubo fought to rise in the church's hierarchy. He wasn't the sort of person to lose his drive after a setback like this.

"Our problems have certainly shrunk since we met to figure out how to deal with Van and Lavender," I remarked.

Esta nodded. "True. That was a nightmare. I've been through my share of scrapes, but that was surely the worst."

"Traitor." Lavender fluttered around Esta's head, raining little flailing attacks on it all over.

"Ha-ha-ha. It all worked out in the end. Real comrades can't just blindly obey. You should think a little more about being a good partner for Van, too, Lavender... Hey, quit it. Don't pull my hair." Esta smiled initially, but as Lavender's assault persisted, she lost patience and shooed the fairy away. Lavender responded by biting her fingers, turning it into a proper squabble.

I never would have thought Esta could get involved in something so childish.

The discussion was completely derailed.

"Wow, I've heard about meetings turning into fracases, but I'd never really experienced it myself." Albert and Rit exchanged a look after my comment.

"I've seen it plenty of times. In Zoltan especially, it is almost the norm," Albert said.

"Me too," Rit agreed. "A lot of strange people end up being adventurers."

I guess my experiences in the Bahamut Knights were different from those of this pair, who'd been more active as adventurers.

Admittedly, there were some problematic older knights whose goal for calling meetings was merely to go drinking, but I never really thought of those as meetings in the first place.

I wasn't great at holding my liquor, so I had wished those functions would stop.

Esta came from a similar background, so this sort of thing was likely a new experience for her.

"I wonder if this kind of rapport is actually a good thing," I said.

"Maybe," Rit answered.

This squabble seemed frivolous, but perhaps the old Hero's party wouldn't have fallen apart had we built this sort of relationship on our journey.

At the very least, Theodora wouldn't have suffered all alone.

✽ ✽ ✽

"Good morning, Big Brother."

"Good morning."

Ruti and Tisse came by the apothecary early the next morning.

"Morning, you two," I replied. "Care for some breakfast?"

"Mhm. I want to have your cooking."

"Yes, thank you."

I prepared a meal for four.

"Good morning, Ruti, Tisse."

"Good morning, Rit."

"Good morning."

After greeting Rit, Ruti and Tisse took spots at the table.

"Today's menu is eggs Benedict, a sauté of cabbage, spinach, and olives, some bacon soup, and berries with yogurt."

I lined up each selection on the table.

"It looks great," Ruti praised.

A poached egg and shrimp on buttered toast, eggs Benedict with asparagus and a lemon sauce—the enticing fusion of colors was also a selling point.

Ruti's eyes gleamed as she beheld the food.

All right, no point in waiting around.

""Let's eat.""

Ruti cut into the eggs Benedict.

"Mm, it's delicious." She smiled happily.

I was glad that she and Tisse got to sample some of the spring vegetables Rit and I had been given.

Together, the four of us made quick work of the remaining greens. Something about that made me happy.

Once finished, I washed the dishes with Ruti.

She offered to take care of it herself, but it was kind of nice to handle it together.

"Here."

"Ah, thanks."

We didn't say much. The only sounds were the clinks of plates and tableware as we cleaned and put them away.

"…" Ruti kept quiet and washed everything earnestly. It was adorable, and she looked happy.

* * *

"I see."

After breakfast, I told Ruti and Tisse that I intended to see Van and Ljubo today. They both nodded and then considered the idea for a moment.

"Do you really plan to investigate the ruins without bringing Ms. Ruti?" Tisse asked.

"Yes, I'd like her to watch things in Zoltan," I replied.

"I don't like it." Ruti's displeasure was evident from how her eyebrows arched. I'd already made up my mind, however.

The secret of the Hero slept in those ancient elf ruins. The first Hero's sacred blade had sent Ruti on a rampage, and although she controlled her old Hero blessing with her New Truth one, I was still a little scared of her getting too close to the secret buried in those old structures.

Plus, Ruti was retired. There was no need for her to go delving after the secret of the Hero anymore. This was an adventure for the new Hero and his party, and for the Guide.

"I don't like it at all. You're my guide. And I want to be with you, Big Brother," Ruti grumbled, puffing out her cheeks.

"But this is Van's adventure. While we're gone, please take care of Zoltan and the shop."

"Mrgh, it's not fair that Rit gets to go."

The expedition group included Van, Lavender, Esta, Albert, Danan, Yarandrala, Rit, and me.

I would lead as a guide, while Rit would fulfill the scout role Van's party lacked. She and I worked best together. Yarandrala would handle support because Ljubo wasn't coming. As for Danan…

"I understand compensating for things missing from Van's party, but why Danan?" Ruti asked.

"Because he's strong."

It truly was that simple. A lot went into balancing a party, but in the end, Danan was just really, really powerful. There was no telling what might appear in the ancient elf ruins, so keeping one tough guy around would make things easier.

In a pinch, we'd rely on Danan. Undoubtedly, he'd make something work.

I counted on him pretty often while we traveled together…

"Since you're not coming, I thought it might be good to have some raw might on the team," I replied.

"That wouldn't be an issue if I came along," Ruti argued.

"Now, now." Rit did her best to placate my sister, but she remained grumpy.

"There's plenty to do on your plantation now that it's spring, right? I bet you've got more customers, too. Just take it easy here in Zoltan this time," I said.

"That's true, but…"

"We'll be back before you know it, and things will be peaceful again. We can go for a walk after this is over."

Ruti nodded, finally accepting. "…Okay. I'll protect Zoltan to enjoy a stroll with you, Big Brother."

"Is it really fine for me to stay behind?" Tisse questioned.

"Hmm," I replied. Having Tisse around would definitely be reassuring. She worked well with others and could fill any role she was given.

"But there are already eight of us. I don't really want the party any larger than that."

The ideal size for an adventuring group was five to six people. That was the optimal number for keeping commands quick and staying on top of everyone's individual predicaments.

However, parties of three or four were more common. Finding five others you were willing to entrust your life to wasn't easy, and coordinating six people could be a challenge. One person could stay out of the fighting and focus on leadership, but that tended to cause arguments. In every country on the continent, there was a strong belief that a commander needed to lead the charge to raise the morale and courage of their troops.

Leaders of the demon lord's army often specialized in their command positions. Were it not for the war, I would have inquired about how they managed to raise soldiers who fought so bravely without their superiors beside them on the front lines.

"Our party was cobbled together at the last minute, and not everyone is used to working together. And Van's party didn't exactly have great teamwork before. I think keeping the party to eight people is best," I said.

"I see. Understood." Tisse bobbed her head, evidently accepting my reasoning.

"But, Big Brother," Ruti began.

"What?"

"Please be careful. God created the Hero, and it wasn't out of compassion for people. As someone with the Divine Blessing of the Hero, I know that much for certain."

"The reason…," I muttered.

"If anything happens, call me. I will absolutely come to help, no matter how far away you are."

"Thanks, Ruti."

She was right. The Hero blessing didn't exist to save people. That's why I wanted Van, who fought for his blessing, to learn the truth.

I didn't want him to regret his journey.

* * *

I stopped by Dr. Newman's clinic to check on Ljubo at around ten in the morning.

"Gideon."

"It's Red here, Your Eminence."

"Hmph. So the hero knight Gideon of Avalonia's Bahamut Knights now works as an apothecary in this backwater of all places."

"Do you mean to imply that I should be out fighting, Your Eminence?"

He shook his head. "No. I cannot understand resigning yourself to a boring job when you could earn more elsewhere. One man won't make a difference in a war that spans the world. Van thinks differently, but I don't believe some tiny town joining the fight will change things. War demands logical thought."

This wasn't the sort of perspective I expected of a holy man. Still, a person who only concerned themselves with appeasing God likely wouldn't have sought to climb the church's ranks, either.

Ljubo had achieved a position only possible for those with the Divine Blessing of the Cardinal. A cardinal was a title only those with the matching blessing could work toward. The rank was one of the highest among the holy church, the world's greatest organization. Those with the Cardinal blessing were willing to do anything to reach that position.

And because that honorable path was open to them, all other routes were closed. I felt a bit of sympathy for those like Ljubo, who were born with the Cardinal blessing.

"Now then, you mentioned taking Van to those ancient elf ruins," Ljubo said.

"Yes."

"I'm not too excited about that. That's where that ancient elf weapon came from, correct?"

We never told Ljubo about Ruti, so he still believed an ancient elf weapon defeated Van.

"That's why Danan and I will accompany him. We don't expect a fight, but we'll be ready should the worst occur," I replied, calmly maintaining the pretense.

"Well, you are the one who stopped Van's reckless rampage. I would prefer to go as well, but I'll entrust this matter to you. I should be able to walk again soon, but it will be some time before I can fight."

Despite nearly dying because of the boy he'd been looking after, Ljubo did not seem to harbor a grudge.

"Aren't you scared of Van or angry with him, Your Eminence?"

"Me? Absurd. Van is the Hero. No matter how misguided he might become or what sins he commits, that does not change the fact that he is the Hero. I am a cardinal of the holy church, which represents God's will. It is my duty to support Van."

I sensed no doubt in his words. He was being genuine.

Ambition and faith.

It reminded me of Ares. What would Ljubo do if Van ever decided to quit?

At the moment, it seemed like Van was at peace with his role, so I guessed things were okay for the time being, but...

At noon, I left the shop to Rit and departed for the meeting place Esta told me about. Supposedly, Van was waiting there.

"This is it."

I checked the note she gave me again.

This is definitely it.

"Tiger Heart sword school."

The building stood in northern Zoltan.

It was a fairly popular school led by the former champion of Zoltan's colosseum. A sign out front advertised, THE INVINCIBLE SWORDS-MANSHIP OF THE UNSHAKABLE CHAMPION JANKO! However, Janko had lost to the current champion, the great hammer-wielder Volga, so the sign's boast felt a little weak.

However, because of the income from his school, Janko could focus his time on the colosseum and not worry about adventuring to earn money. He couldn't afford to change the sign.

Realizing my thoughts were straying, I refocused myself.

What was Van the Hero doing at a lowly sword academy?

Is he going around challenging masters of various styles?

No one in any other town or city would care.

"Guess I'll go in."

The door to the school was closed.

After making sure no one was around, I leaped over the fence and snuck inside.

"Please!"

"O-okay! I will be your partner for overhead defense practice!"

Van's spirited voice was met with a shrill reply.

Peeking into the room, I saw Van looking serious and holding a wooden sword, and a man who seemed on the verge of tears.

The man was probably a teacher here. The other gathered students were quiet, and their eyes were watery as well. Tiger Heart Janko, former champion of Zoltan's colosseum, watched Van with moist eyes hidden behind his bushy white eyebrows.

Teaching your techniques to someone so strong that they could kill you in an instant had to be one of the most painful things for a swordsman.

"Hah! Hah! Hah!" Van shouted, while the Tiger Heart–style instructor brandished his wooden sword without any trace of actual fighting spirit.

"Oh, he's taking this seriously," I muttered.

Van earnestly mirrored the fundamental defensive basics. These were the sorts of techniques a student of two to three months would practice. Van had focused too heavily on his blessing and ignored proper swordsmanship, but he should have learned the basics of combat from the church, and that included practical defensive techniques.

"That's probably more his natural style," I muttered.

Were it not for the miracle that changed Van's blessing from the Cardinal to the Hero, he would have grown into a serious and earnest cleric.

I watched for a while as he repeated that basic movement.

Once the practice began to wind down, I stepped into the room.

Van perked up. "Ah, Gi—"

"Red."

"Right, Red!"

Van hurried over to me.

The students of the school breathed a sigh of relief, glad to be free of the Hero.

"I went to see Cardinal Ljubo earlier. He's quite resilient. In another few days, he should be able to walk again," I said.

"I go to see him every day... He has every right to blame me for my loss of control, yet he merely says he's glad I realized my sin."

Van was crucial to Ljubo's plans for himself. The Cardinal would never abandon the Hero, even if Van went on a rampage.

Never had I felt so glad to live a simple life as an apothecary.

"You forgave me, too, even though I hurt you. I wouldn't blame you for holding a grudge, you know," Van said.

"Oh, right."

I did get cut pretty badly during our fight. Ruti had healed me immediately after, so there wasn't even a scar, but ordinarily, I would have died.

"But I hurt you, too," I replied. "We dueled; it happens. There's no point to staying bitter over a duel."

"Oh, really?"

Van probably couldn't understand yet. However, his acknowledging that others would bear him ill will because he hurt them was progress. The old Van might have said something about how they ought to be grateful for being wounded for the sake of divine blessings. Any indication that Van saw people instead of blessings was a step in the right direction.

"Anyway, I thought we could head to the ancient elf ruins tomorrow morning," I said.

"Finally…!" There was a mixture of anticipation and unease in his eyes.

"If you're worried, we can always abandon the idea."

"No, I want to go. If I can learn why I was given the Divine Blessing of the Hero, I know it will make me stronger. I'll be able to stand tall and fight proudly as the Hero."

Van looked uneasy but confident. He seemed like a genuine human being instead of the slave to his blessing he was previously.

Van remained worried about some things, but he wasn't lost in the way he had been. Thus, I needed only to guide him to what he sought.

"You know, I didn't think you'd visit a sword school," I said.

"I started two days ago. I wanted to learn the basics before your lessons."

Right. I'd promised to teach him a bit while we were on the road.

"So that's why."

"I don't know how much time it will take to explore the ancient elf ruins, but I'm sure it won't be that long."

"Yeah, the plan is to return after a week at most."

"I don't have much time to learn bladework, so I became a short-term pupil at the most well-known school here in Zoltan," Van explained.

This was the most famous sword school around, although some had doubts as to if it was the best. I hadn't sparred with any of the teachers in Zoltan, so I couldn't say for sure, but an academy that taught a style from Central was probably better quality. Tiger Heart–style was popular because Janko had made a name for himself in the colosseum.

Well, the basics are universal across disciplines, I guess.

"Hey, let's move this conversation to somewhere else," I said.

"…?" Van cocked his head.

"You should probably learn to pay a bit more attention to your surroundings."

The students stared at me. A downtown apothecary was speaking casually with Van the Hero.

It was only natural that they wanted to know why.

People in Zoltan already knew that I was actually fairly strong, but even so, it was better to change the location before people got too suspicious.

"All right," Van replied. "Let me speak with Mr. Janko first, since he's been so helpful."

"Yeah. You should thank him for the lessons."

This was Van's last day here. Now those shuddering students would be free.

※   ※   ※

"Please wait!" a voice called to Van and me right as we left the school. Turning around, we saw Janko himself. He was trembling, and he gritted his teeth as he stood before us.

"What is it, Mr. Janko?" Van asked.

Janko's face was ghostly pale as he all but shouted, "Van the Hero! I would like to spar with you just once, please!"

""Huh?""

Van and I were both stunned.

A match with Van?!

"M-Master! What are you saying?!"

Students hurried to their teacher, frantically trying to stop him.

Despite my earlier remarks about Janko, he was among the top ten swordsmen in Zoltan. Yet he had no chance of matching Van the Hero.

"I won't forget your teachings, and I am grateful for them...but I don't think it would be a real fight between the two of us." Van offered the middle-aged instructor the simple truth with a boyish innocence.

"I know full well my sword has no chance of victory... If I kept silent, I could return to being a simple master in Zoltan." Janko shook as he spoke. "But today is the only chance I'll ever get to spar with you! This moment, right now! This is my only chance to cross swords with the Hero! The world's strongest! As a swordsman, I would regret it for the rest of my life if I held back now!"

Master of a small-time school or not, Janko was still a warrior.

"Red." Van looked to me.

"So long as you don't have any issues with it, why not indulge him?" I said.

Van looked like he didn't get why Janko wanted to fight. "Understood. Then please, sir."

That was his answer.

As expected, the fight was over in an instant.

Van easily evaded Janko's slash, and his attack landed on the older man's torso.

I quickly gave Janko a potion to help him recover.

Van had used a Merciful potion on his sword to make it nonlethal, but his strike still inflicted the kind of pain that could kill someone from shock. Janko had risked his life by asking for a match.

Even after I fed him a cure potion, he remained unconscious.

He likely wouldn't wake up soon, yet I couldn't help but think he looked satisfied.

A battle he never expected had found him in Zoltan. For a swordsman, there was perhaps no greater stroke of good fortune.

"Why did he want to fight me?" Van wondered.

"You'll understand one day if you keep practicing," I replied.

"Really…?"

If I had to boil down the difference between a swordsman and a fighter who carried a sword, it was that the weapon itself became the swordsman's goal. The swordsman saw value in their style and techniques. Their blade wasn't merely a tool for fighting. The true devotees to the sword wondered how well their attacks would fare against the world's strongest and what an opponent like that was capable of.

"Even though he lost…he seems pleased."

"Yeah. Be proud, Van. You fulfilled a man's impossible dream."

Van still didn't seem to understand.

※　　　　　※　　　　　※

After arranging everything for tomorrow with Van, I informed Yarandrala and Danan of the plans on my way back. Yarandrala still despised the Hero, but Danan had accepted Van's reform quickly and tried to placate the elf.

Knowing the two of them, it'd be fine.

With everything set, we were ready to depart whenever.

Following a late lunch at a food stall, I headed to my final stops for the day.

I met Galatine from the Adventurers Guild along the way and informed him that the incident with Van had been resolved without issue.

I also visited Gonz and Tanta and promised to take a day off to sail a boat down the river in a couple of weeks.

Peaceful days had returned to Zoltan.

The last errand was at Drake's Armory.

"Red, eh? Don't tell me you broke your sword again!"

Mogrim greeted me as he often did. I'd only recently bought the bronze sword that shattered during the fight with Van, so I understood where he was coming from.

"…And that's the situation. Do you have any bronze swords in stock?"

"If you go around breakin' 'em like twigs, I'm not sure I want to keep selling them!"

Glancing at the angry dwarf, I fished through a bin of cheap, used, and mass-produced weapons.

"Huh? There are no bronze swords here."

"I ran out because you keep breaking them all."

"I haven't broken enough to exhaust your stock!"

Mogrim heaved a sigh.

"It's the time of year when new adventurers start poppin' up. A bunch of kids bought them up recently. I'm fresh out."

"I see…"

This was a catastrophe.

"How about buying a normal weapon?" Mogrim suggested. "I can make you one the same size as a bronze sword."

"No, I need it right away."

"Then pick a sword off the wall! Cheap swords are dangerous, so I don't want you using one of them!"

"Your bronze sword cut through the skin of that gem beast. If it can hold against a monster like that, then it'll be fine no matter what I face."

The legendary gem beast we fought at the Wall at the End of the World—a remnant created by the ancient elves.

Mogrim gnashed his teeth. "Don't go twistin' things! Just listen to your smith when it concerns weapons!"

Mogrim was a crafting specialist, and he really didn't like me risking my life with a low-quality tool like a bronze sword.

I understood the feeling, but…

"Hahhh," Mogrim sighed. "If I refuse, you're just going to buy one somewhere else, aren't you?"

"Yeah."

"Fine, then. Wait a bit."

Mogrim went into the back of the shop.

After a few minutes, he came out holding a sheathed, one-handed sword.

"Here, a bronze sword."

"So you had one after all."

I took it from him and inspected the blade. Its sharp gleam suggested craftsmanship of a level that left me dubious as to whether it genuinely was a bronze sword.

"Who tempers a bronze sword to this level?" I asked.

"Hmph. On a whim, I got curious about how far I could enhance a bronze sword. So I gave it a shot. That's all."

Mogrim had grown tired of me buying cheap blades, so he decided to create a bronze sword with a proper edge. Crafting a fine weapon out of steel would have been far easier, making this a very roundabout kind of sword.

Ah. So it's a pretty good fit for me.

"I'm not havin' a comrade die 'cause of my handiwork. With this, you can cut down as many monsters around Zoltan as you like, and you won't find a single crack in the blade."

"Thank you, I'll buy it."

Using a bronze sword was part of my style. Perhaps you could call it a pointless obsession.

Mogrim was kind enough to satisfy my conviction with his own as a blacksmith.

I need to take good care of this weapon.

"Don't go doin' something stupid like dying tryin' to save that sword. If it breaks, I'll make another."

Urk. He saw right through me.

Mogrim was a good sort.

✻ ✻ ✻

With all my work finished for the day, I was free to return home.

Both of my hands were full with purchases for exploring the ruins.

An adventurer was always prepared.

"I'm back."

"Welcome home, Red!"

"Welcome home, Big Brother."

Rit and Ruti both greeted me when I came in. When I took my coat off, Rit grabbed it for me.

"It's pretty hot out. I could've gone without a jacket," I remarked.

"Summer's on the way, after all," Rit said.

When I sat down, Ruti brought me a cup of water from the kitchen.

"Here, Big Brother."

"Thanks."

I'd started to sweat a bit outside, so the water was nice.

"How did it go?" Rit asked.

"Everything's set. We're heading out tomorrow."

"I see. It's exciting, exploring ancient elf ruins!" Rit sounded pleased. I guess her adventurer's blood was stirring. That was reassuring.

"You know." I took another sip of water. "I feel like I've talked to a lot of different people these past couple of days."

Each of them had their firm convictions.

Were I still the man I was upon first arriving in Zoltan, the one who'd lost his only purpose in life, those people wouldn't have meant much to me.

However, spending more time with Rit and Ruti opened my eyes. I recognized that everyone had their passions and met them with my own.

"Maybe that's a bit overly sentimental, though," I mused quietly with a wry smile.

Van and his party would depart Zoltan once we were done with the ancient elf ruins. Danan intended to leave, too. And there was no telling how long Yarandrala would remain. I was just a small supporting player in their grand stories.

But that was fine.

Hearing tales of their heroic exploits someday was enough for me.

And if they ever felt like stopping by Zoltan sometime to share a story or two, I'd be proud to know I'd played a part.

""Welcome!""

A customer entered, and Rit and Ruti greeted them cheerfully.

This was my home.

Chapter 2
Dungeon Crawl

We reached the entrance to the ancient elf ruins in the mountains by the evening.

The surrounding area was home to chimeras—creatures with a lion body and head, plus a dragon and goat head.

That was fine, though. They weren't really any trouble for us. Rit marched at the head of our group and thus was the one beset upon by a chimera that leaped at us. However, the monster was taken down in an instant, and the rest of its kind left us alone. Other than that, it was smooth sailing.

As planned, the party totaled eight people: Rit, Yarandrala, Danan, Van, Lavender, Esta, Albert, and myself.

"The real exploration will start tomorrow, but there is an area inside that was used as a base last time, so let's move there before we stop for the night," I said.

Everyone nodded.

Ruti had set up that section of the ruins for Godwin. The camp remained, even after the battle with Ares.

"So this is an ancient elf ruin." Van touched the unknown metal that formed a wall with evident fascination.

"Is this your first time exploring one?" I asked.

"Mhm. The clockwork constructs here lack Divine Blessings, and no evil comes from them."

"True, there are no people for the Hero to rescue down here," I replied. The ancient elf ruins were irrelevant to that role. And yet they were deeply linked to its origins. "But Ruti found the proof of the Hero in an ancient elf ruin."

Esta pulled the item in question out of her pocket. "Here."

"What?!" Van cried out. "Why do you have that, Esta?!"

"I received it from Lady Ruti."

Ruti said she'd thrown it away when she abandoned her quest and came to Zoltan. I guess Esta picked it up.

"It does nothing for me, though," she admitted.

"Because it's meant to enhance the Divine Blessing of the Hero," I said.

Our exchange got Van thinking. "Enhancing a Divine Blessing... That doesn't feel right for the Hero..."

"True," I agreed.

A magic item that directly enhanced a Divine Blessing was extraordinarily rare. Blessings were quite literally gifts from God. Manipulating a blessing by mortal means was heretical, and openly researching such things was forbidden. Even if it was allowed, the subject was beyond what modern mages could achieve.

Knowing that Devil's Blessing existed, perhaps it was possible with techniques from the dark continent. On Avalon, the only ones able to manipulate blessings were the wild elves, who were said to be descendants of the ancient elves. The extinct wood elves, modern half-elves, and high elves lacked the knowledge to affect blessings.

"Elven coins are the same." Yarandrala pulled out a platinum coin.

Those, too, were ancient elven artifacts made of an unknown metal.

When Rit first started living with me, a man from the Thieves Guild tried to buy me off with one of those.

Appearance suggested it was merely a piece of old currency, but by unleashing its power, you could increase your blessing level by one. It was a bit of a waste to use something worth ten thousand payrils like that, but we'd expended them regularly in the old days before fights with mighty foes.

Not dying was worth more than money.

"You can find them all over the place in ancient elven ruins, and there are plenty of other powerful artifacts, too. Whenever we had time to spare, and there was an ancient elven ruin nearby, we explored it," I said.

"I always thought raising my blessing level took precedence over everything else," Van confessed. Some of that was probably because of Ljubo. Was it best to grow strong by raising your blessing level or seeking to improve your skills and equipment? Whatever the true answer, Ljubo's perspective as a holy man and mine as a knight clearly differed.

"Speaking of the proof of the Hero, how much do you know of the legends of the Ancient Hero, Van?" I asked.

"I have read everything in the records left in the church, of course."

"So on that front, you're a model student."

Ruti had absolutely no interest in the Ancient Hero, since she despised the Hero blessing. However, Ares, Esta, and I all knew the legends, so with comrades able to cover for her on the knowledge front, there hadn't been a problem.

"The story of the Ancient Hero obtaining the proof of the Hero came after Sage Lilith decided to join the Ancient Hero's quest because she was impressed by his spirit," Van recounted. "Lilith was a scholar of antiquity. She studied the Heroes who lived before the era of humanity; the ones lost to modern history and legends. She concluded that they visited an ancient elven structure near the capital of the present-day Kingdom of Avalonia. Lilith guided the Hero of her time to those ruins, and there, they discovered the proof of the Hero. Only the Hero may acquire that treasure, which leads to people acknowledging anyone with it as God's chosen savior and gathering to him to fight the demon lord's army."

The Ancient Hero. The one who defeated the demon lord and began the age of humans.

Unlike the modern Heroes—Ruti and Van—his journey began after the demon lord seized control of the entire world. The wood elves, who'd dominated the continent at the time, fought the demon lord's army but were destroyed. It was said that the various human kingdoms and tribes were forced to accept the demon lord as their master and live under the thumb of demons.

That was when the Ancient Hero appeared, although his name had since been lost. Together with his comrades, he stoked rebellion in every corner of the continent, then finally invaded the demon lord's castle and defeated the tyrant.

Later, the Ancient Hero married Sage Lilith, and their son united humanity as ruler of its first kingdom, Gaiapolis. The great warrior Maharaj established the Warriors Guild—what would later become the Adventurers Guild. The cleric Corsica was central in rebuilding the holy church. All the heroes in the party had their hands in modern institutions.

But ironically, the Kingdom of Gaiapolis was later destroyed by the descendants of the humans exiled for having joined the demon lord's army.

That land later became mine and Ruti's homeland, the Kingdom of Avalonia. Its capital stood on the former site of the Hero's castle in Gaiapolis, which itself had rested on the land the demon lord's palace once occupied.

"As a result of all that chaos, the records of the Ancient Hero were lost," Rit said with evident disappointment.

Esta nodded in agreement. "The church and the Avalonian archives are similarly incomplete. The only hope would be the historical records of the Cataphract Kingdom, which was founded by the remnants of Gaiapolis's royal family. However, if such knowledge survived, Cataphract would have no reason to conceal it. It surely would have announced it, advertising that it knew the true lineage of the Hero."

Thus, despite the Ancient Hero's great feats, we didn't know what sort of person he was or even his name.

But was that really it?

The names of his party members endured. Part of that was because their feats had been recorded by the organizations they founded, but why was there no mention of the greatest Hero's name? I sensed a hidden motive in the conspicuous lack of knowledge about the Hero.

Whether it was malicious or well-intentioned was another question, however.

* * *

We entered the ancient elf ruins and reached the elevator area. This was as far as Zoltan adventurers dared to go.

Many plants grew to this point. Perhaps it was a good environment, as there were lots of medicinal herbs to be found. Those bold adventurers unafraid of the chimeras came here to do some gathering. No one ventured past the elevator, though.

"Shall we go down?" I peered down the hole. "Do you have a way to descend safely, Van?"

"Of course!"

"All right, then, shall we?"

Everyone leaped into the hole.

I kicked off the walls to slow my descent. Beside me, Rit used her spirit magic to descend slowly. Esta also used magic, albeit a little more unstably because she was holding Albert.

With her abilities, she should have been able to control the fall just fine, even with another person. She looked a little unsteady, though, so I signaled for Rit and Yarandrala to support her.

As for Van, he simply ran straight down the wall.

"Van's fastest!" Lavender cheered excitedly from his shoulder.

It's not really a race…

"Don't get cocky!" Danan raced down the shaft. He used Martial Arts to accelerate in midair. And just before slamming into the ground, he managed to slow himself to land safely.

He really was superhuman.

"How's that?"

"That stupid musclehead! Getting in Van's way!"

"You're amazing, Danan."

Danan was triumphant, Lavender resentful, and Van observed things in his own way. The rest of us landed in succession shortly after the three of them.

Everyone was safe.

"The base is this way."

I took the lead, guiding the party. Rit, our scout, was up front beside me. The rest took positions at our backs.

After a little while...

"Hmm?"

...I stopped walking, sensing something strange. There'd been clockwork constructs guarding these ruins, but Ruti had destroyed them; their remnants were ahead.

"What is it, Red?" Rit asked.

"Can you wait just a moment?"

I took a closer look at the remnants.

There's not enough.

"Parts are missing. Someone must have taken them."

"Huh? But no one has come in here since the last time, right?" Rit sounded surprised. "I don't think there are any adventurers who would dare venture into ancient elf ruins. Plus, there weren't any signs of other people at the entrance!"

I nodded. "I didn't notice anything that would suggest other parties passing through, either."

Rit's Spirit Scout abilities and Yarandrala's Singer of the Trees abilities were connected to plants.

The entrance to the ruins was carpeted in vegetation like an overgrown forest. An adventuring group would have to go to great lengths to avoid leaving any evidence of their presence in the vegetation that those two would recognize. Such a thing was beyond anyone in Zoltan.

"Perhaps there's another entrance?" Van suggested.

That was certainly a possibility.

"I think there probably is another entrance. But if adventurers had come here, then it's odd that they left the clockwork constructs' armor plating. Those are the most valuable pieces," I replied.

"I see. Hmmm…"

Van's brow knitted in thought.

Maybe—

"What pointless thing are you worrying about now?" Lavender said before I could speak up. "They cannibalize themselves, right? I've seen it tons of times."

That wasn't a hypothesis; she'd witnessed it.

Right…

"You were alive during the ancient elves' era," I said.

Lavender was an archfay of calamity.

According to Undine, she was the last of the archfay of calamity who once rampaged across the world but were brought low by the dragons and ancient elves.

All that time spent trying to study ancient elves, and a firsthand source is now right in front of me.

"What's it matter? It was so long ago."

Unfortunately, Lavender didn't seem interested in talking about the ancient elves.

She didn't really distinguish between different people for the most part, so she'd probably fail to recall much about the ancient elves.

Fairies really had a different set of priorities than people.

"Cannibalizing? They eat?"

It sounded like Danan had misunderstood entirely.

"They gather usable parts from broken constructs to fix other clockwork monsters," I explained.

"Meaning…?"

"Basically, we should be careful because new clockwork constructs might show up."

"Ohhh! Just say that from the start, man!" Danan grinned and slapped my back.

Cut it out. That hurts, you know.

I didn't really understand that much about clockworks, either. They were geared monsters that functioned for thousands of years, operating ceaselessly since the era of their creators. Researchers tried to forge copies of them using current-day magic and engineering, but no amount of study produced anything like what these golems could manage.

"Clockwork monsters can be dangerous. They give off a sound when they move, but otherwise, their presence can't be detected, even by magic," Rit said.

"They don't breathe and have no body heat, so it's difficult even using the plants," Yarandrala added.

You could do nothing against a surprise attack by clockwork golems other than try to fight back after you were caught.

Tisse had told me that the defensive fortifications of these ruins were extraordinary. They were enough to make her admit she wouldn't have returned alive without Ruti.

"Apparently, there was even a clockwork dragon somewhere down here. We'll need to take care, as it might have been restored," I said.

"A clockwork dragon… That's a monster that appears in the legend of the Ancient Hero," Van replied.

"Yeah, the ancient demon lord's army restored it and used it for war. I don't know if the one here possesses the same abilities as the one in the old stories, but it will surely be a dangerous opponent, even for the Hero."

Come to think of it, legends of the Ancient Hero only spoke of ancient elf technology during the part about the proof of the Hero and when mentioning that the demon lord's army restored the machines and set them against humanity.

Maybe that's part of why Van—the church's Hero—and his party put so little emphasis on ancient elven ruins.

"Hey, Lavender, who were the ancient elves?" I asked.

"Who were they? Just normal animals, the same as you humans."

She regarded me as though wondering why I'd bothered to ask the obvious.

I had a font of information right before me, but apparently, I'd need to work a little harder to get what I wanted from her.

"That's enough, right? Let's keep going so we can get some rest soon," Danan suggested.

"Yeah, good call."

With that, we continued deeper toward Ruti's abandoned camp.

✳   ✳   ✳

We proceeded with caution, and fortunately, we managed to avoid any clockwork constructs that might be roaming the halls.

The sounds of shoes on the metallic floor echoed down the otherwise silent passage.

We marched to where that odd sign with HERO ADMINISTRATION BUREAU written on it in wood elf script was and beyond.

"This is the place," I said.

At last, we'd reached the chamber that Godwin the Alchemist used as a laboratory.

"The door's broken," Van remarked.

I nodded. "That was Ruti."

"You don't say."

I felt partly responsible, but we were the only ones who'd use the room anyway, so it was fine. I could imagine some scholar in the distant future getting mad at whoever had broken the things in their precious ruins, but I decided not to think too deeply about it.

"So then, shall we set up camp?" I asked.

Van reached for his item box. "Mhm. Leave it to me. I have a handy magic item that Ljubo—"

"Slow down there," I interjected. "Since we have the chance, why not try setting up camp yourself without using a magic item?"

"Huh?! Why?!"

"During all your travels, you've relied on magic items or let members of the church who were with you handle everything, right?"

"That's true, but is there a reason to go out of the way to do it by hand when it can be done quicker?"

"What will you do when you find yourself unable to use magic items? What if your item box gets stolen? Someday, you might get thrown in prison with just the shirt on your back, forcing you to break out and reunite with your comrades."

"...I understand."

"All right, here's everything you'll need. See what you can do with Esta's guidance."

Van reluctantly went over to Esta. She smiled wryly at him but launched into an earnest explanation.

Rit came up beside me. "He's pretty obedient."

"He's serious and a hard worker at heart. If he learns to accept other people's perspectives, he'll be much better off. I think his old mentality, when he took his faith too far, isn't his natural personality."

"Hmm. Blessings are difficult things."

"They really are. I wonder what Demis hoped to achieve by making the Hero."

If the goal was to defeat the demon lord and save the world, there were plenty of more efficient ways to go about it. The Divine Blessing of the Hero did not exist to save the world.

"Ruti and Van are completely different Heroes, but they both agree on that point," I said.

"You're right about that," Rit answered.

Ruti claimed that the Hero wasn't made to save people, and Van asserted that the Hero wasn't meant to defeat evil so much as just battle it regardless of the outcome.

And the words of two people who possessed the Hero blessing were more reliable than any old legend.

"Does Demis view good and evil as equal?" Rit pondered aloud. "I wonder if he created Divine Blessings of equal strength so one side wouldn't have an edge over the other."

I shook my head. "That doesn't feel quite right. Were that true, the Hero and the demon lord would be unnecessary. Ordinary people and demons would be enough."

"Yeah. It would be amazing if we could find an answer here."

"Even if we do, who knows if what we'll find can be revealed to the public? It's probably a good thing that Ljubo didn't come with us."

While we talked, Van and Esta finished setting up camp. There was no need to deal with wind or rain, so there was no tent, but there were cots and a simple kitchen area. We'd be set for a few days.

"Nice work," I praised.

"It's not hard as long as you know what you are doing." Van sounded a little proud of his work. In that regard, he really was like an innocent boy.

"Shall we have some dinner, then?" I suggested.

And just like that, our first day of adventure concluded unremarkably.

* * *

Although it was night, there was no sun or moon underground.

After dinner, the others spent their time as they pleased. I was teaching Van swordsmanship with a practice weapon.

"You're open."

"Ngh!"

The blade of my sword stopped just a hair from Van's nape.

We were taking care not to actually hit each other, as this was practice to improve Van's form. In a scenario where all of Van's powerful skills from his blessing could only hasten the speed of his weapon, I had a pretty considerable advantage.

"Okay, let's work on defending when you're rooted and can't move."

"Yes, sir!"

Van earnestly parroted all the motions I taught him. He was a good student.

"You have a habit of trying to finish things with special Hero maneuvers. And you aren't great at applying practical motions," I said.

"So what should I do?"

"I'd say work to find different ways of using your Hero abilities. Something to repel an opponent's attacks without losing the upper hand would be useful."

"Ohhh!"

Swordsmanship wasn't mastered in a day; that was especially true because Van had already formed many bad practices from so much fighting. However, the more he practiced, the more he picked up the motions. At present, he likely felt weaker than before. It would be hard to fight while keeping the principles I taught in mind. But he would surely grow even stronger than before in time.

"*Phew*, let's call it there for today."

"Aww. But..."

Van looked like he wanted more, but it was eleven. We'd been going for too long already, honestly.

"Can't we continue a bit more?"

Until recently, Van didn't see any value in swordsmanship. Yet now he'd come to understand how interesting it could be.

"I only have a short amount of time to teach you the sword, but once you resume your journey, you should take care to observe how others fight. There are as many different styles as there are sword fighters. It's fun," I replied.

I sat down and wiped my dirty body with a wet towel. "Now then, you have Immunity to Sleep, don't you?"

"Mhm. That's why I always spend nights hunting monsters to raise my blessing level."

"And I go with him!"

Lavender had cheered for Van during training and zipped to his shoulder once it was over.

"Then until I go to sleep, let's talk a little more about the Ancient

Hero and the proof of the Hero," I said as I set the towel down. "Van, do you know what happened to the original proof of the Hero?"

"According to the church's records, it was returned to the ancient elf ruins after the demon lord was defeated."

"That's right. But why did the Ancient Hero do that?"

Van was at a loss for a moment. "In order to entrust it to the next Hero?"

"That's a nice idea. There was something in the ruins where we recovered the proof of the Hero that prevented it from being taken by anyone without the Divine Blessing of the Hero. I can't think of any better way to ensure that the next Hero is the one to make the trip. Until I traveled with Ruti, I thought like you did."

"Huh?"

"Van, do you think the Hero's impulses will stop after the demon lord is defeated? Will that mean the end of the blessing's purpose?"

"...Ah!"

"The Hero is meant to defeat evil and save people. So long as there is evil in the world and people in danger, the Hero's work will never be done. Expunging all wickedness and danger is impossible."

Slaying the demon lord wouldn't free Ruti from her impulses. My dream, a future where she could live in peace like an ordinary girl, wouldn't come true with the demon lord's demise.

"I see. It's strange that the Ancient Hero returned the proof of the Hero after defeating the demon lord," Van said.

"That's right. The Hero's role was not yet complete, so he shouldn't have quit. He still needed the proof of the Hero."

"Hmmm..." Van thought about it, but it didn't seem like he reached an answer.

I poured a cup of coffee and waited for it to cool down before resuming the conversation.

"My theory is that he never returned the proof of the Hero."

Van raised an eyebrow. "That doesn't make any sense."

"Hear me out. We know that Sage Lilith was a hero who saved the world, and she was the mother of the royal lineage that ruled the continent. But originally, she was a scholar of antiquity. She must have known about ancient elf ruins."

I paused and took a sip of coffee.

A bit bitter... Did I mess up grinding the beans?

"I've done quite a lot of research on the ancient elves, too," I added.

I'd searched far and wide for a way to restrain the impulses of Ruti's blessing. I even sought out ancient elf and demon practices. Ultimately, I never found a way to free her, but I did learn things that wound up being useful during our travels.

Most importantly, that knowledge of ancient elves taught me about a different world than the one the church spoke of.

"When we found the proof of the Hero in the ancient elf ruins near the capital, the item was made new there. It was nothing more than a freshly produced ancient elf creation, totally distinct from the one held by the Ancient Hero. It was entirely unrelated to Demis, the creator of the Divine Blessing of the Hero."

"You said that back in the fairy village, too, but...I still can't believe it. It is written in the church's scriptures that the proof of the Hero was crafted of the divine metal orichalcum and thus bequeathed to us by God."

"Just like this floor." I tapped my hand on the ground, producing a dull noise. "Orichalcum is just a metal we don't know how to make. It's hardly divine. It's a substance fabricated by the ancient elves.

"In other words, the ancient elves understood secrets about the Divine Blessing of the Hero. It's why Sage Lilith's accounts of the Ancient Hero are incomplete. She wished to conceal the truth about the ancient elves."

Sage Lilith used the Hero's lineage to found a kingdom and rule the entire continent. Perhaps she'd come across a truth that threatened her commanding position.

"It's an incredible theory, but I don't think I can put much trust in it," Van said.

"Of course, it's just speculation, after all. Hopefully, we'll find the answer here."

"It's strange. Were I not the Hero, I'd probably be scared right now."

"What will you do? Go back without learning what the Hero is?"

"No. I want to know. I want to learn why I was given this blessing and discover what sort of hero I should be. Then I can save the world." Van's reply was firm and steady.

"That's right!" Lavender chirped. She'd been listening to my story from Van's shoulder with clear disinterest. Now that it was over, she kissed Van's cheek lightly. "You're already the strongest hero. I don't know about that secret or whatever, but you will definitely be fine as long as you stay yourself!"

Van's eyes rested on the little fairy. "Thank you, Lavender."

Before, it always seemed like he looked at Lavender without actually seeing her. Even his comrades had been mere blessings to him. That would change going forward. He would build strong bonds with them.

The two of them started talking cheerfully, so I headed over to my sleeping bag to avoid getting in their way.

"Nice work today."

"You too."

Yarandrala came over and gave me a small bunch of berries. The fruits had a hint of sweetness and tartness to them, making them perfect for a snack.

"To think that the Hero could relax this much," Yarandrala remarked as she observed Van laughing at Lavender's joke. "He might actually be able to save the world."

"Yeah."

"I still can't accept a lone Hero shouldering the world's burdens, though."

Yarandrala had always held that belief. Even during her time in our party, she disliked the Hero's role. Our group really had a wide range of thoughts on humanity's strongest blessing.

"Van belongs to the church," I said. "I'm sure they're abusing that to some extent, but it also means he'll lead the church's army into battle. He won't have to go it alone the entire time. At least, I hope so."

"It all comes down to the blessing's impulses."

"Yeah, it does."

An army couldn't take most of the actions necessary to save people, and the Hero blessing's impulses were a bad fit for such a massive collective. There was a good chance Van would eventually leave the army and try to bear the fate of the world with a small group of people, just like we did.

"Hey, Red." Yarandrala paused to lower her voice. "How come Van can laugh and smile?"

Ruti couldn't. That was what Yarandrala was getting at.

"...I don't know."

That was all I could say in response.

* * *

Breakfast on the second day of our adventure was vegetable-and-egg sandwiches and bacon soup.

I'd prepared some fresh food yesterday for this morning.

The meal was hardly leisurely, but everyone did seem to enjoy it well enough.

Once we finished, we began discussing what to do today.

"Let's split up to search," Danan suggested. "We don't know what might be skulking around, but Ruti and Tisse already explored most of the area, right? We can spread out some until we find something strange."

"Mhm, that sounds good to me! Me and Van together, and everyone else can just do whatever! You want to be together with Red, don't you, Rit?" Lavender said.

"Huh? Well, I did plan to go with Red, but..."

"Lavender, we're having a serious discussion right now."

"Mrgh! I was being serious, Van!"

Lavender's boisterous outburst gave a lightness to the meeting. She would provide a bit of brightness to the grim road Van would head down in the future. However, there was a time and place for her antics.

"Quiet! Let's hear what everyone thinks," I called.

Everyone stopped talking. Lavender tried to keep speaking, but Van put his finger over her lips. She tried to mumble through it, though.

"Ruti and Tisse explored a broad area of these ruins and took care of anything dangerous, but their goal wasn't to discover the secrets of this place. Some of the clockwork constructs may have recovered." I looked around at everyone. "We should split into two parties. I think dividing any more than that would be too risky."

"I agree," Esta said. "And it would be best to keep our searches close enough that either party can rush over if something happens. So sticking to the same floor is better."

I took out signal whistles from my item box and passed them out to everyone. These were common tools used by adventurers; they were small whistles that could produce loud noises at different pitches, letting you signal a comrade at a significant distance.

"Is that agreeable to everyone?" I asked.

Danan nodded. "Yeah, no problem here!"

No one else had any objections.

"So as for the groups…"

Rit, Danan, Yarandrala, and I formed Party A. Van, Lavender, Esta, and Albert would be Party B.

"For now, it's probably better to stick with familiar comrades," I said. "Signal immediately if anything happens. There's no need to go overboard."

"I understand." Van bobbed his head.

He sure is getting to be reliable.

We started by reconfirming the safety of the area that Ruti had explored the last time. This included inspecting where the clockwork mother controlling the other golems had been. It was still broken.

Without it, the clockwork golems shouldn't be able to move, but…

"An army that collapses without its commander?" I muttered.

If I were an ancient elf creating these constructs, I wouldn't implement such an obvious weakness. I would absolutely consider the possibility of the commander falling.

"Well, maybe it was necessary since the clockwork golems aren't living creatures," I mused.

At any rate, we needed to get on with our search.

The day proceeded without incident or results. There were no signs of any changes in the area Ruti had already covered.

Starting tomorrow, we'd have to head down a floor.

* * *

Day three.

Today's breakfast was meat and vegetables grilled in olive oil.

Sopping up the leftover bits of olive oil with some bread proved delicious.

Today, we extended our search to the lower floors.

We went to the room where we fought Ares and where the Sacred Avenger, which Shisandan used, had been stored. I was a little concerned about Van entering the room since he had the Hero blessing and this was where Ruti went berserk, so I investigated the chamber myself.

I was surprised to find a massive magic device I'd never seen before, but I didn't turn up anything related to the Hero. However, the room was a vault for sacred swords; it was hard to imagine it being used for anything else.

Today was another swing and a miss.

* * *

Day four.

Breakfast was a stew made from salt-preserved rations.

We headed up a floor from where we'd made camp.

This level was completely empty.

There were a few more unknown devices, but they all seemed to be broken. The higher floors appeared to have been aboveground at one point. We came upon something that had likely moved to those levels long ago. However, it had long since been buried, making it inoperable.

Today was another failure.

∗   ∗   ∗

Day five.

Breakfast was cookies and bean soup.

We ventured to the last areas we hadn't explored…but found nothing.

We'd been everywhere.

With that done, we gathered again for another meeting shortly after noon.

"There was nothing," Rit said disappointedly.

This was a weak showing. I didn't think it would be so fruitless.

"Did the wood elves just put some joke on that sign?" Danan wondered.

"Hmm. It was presumably written by wood elves who explored these ruins, but there's no guarantee it's accurate," Esta responded.

"Should we follow the typical strategy and have the parties swap routes to see if either group missed something?" Yarandrala suggested, calling upon her wealth of experience as an adventurer.

It was a common method when splitting up. It was even taught during Adventurers Guild training. Everyone had their quirks and habits when it came to searching, so having a second party check sometimes revealed things that'd been overlooked.

"Sounds boring. Should I just break it all?"

"Doesn't that sort of defeat the purpose of this?"

Van looked a bit exasperated as he gently shot down Lavender's proposal.

Breaking everything was out of the question. There was almost certainly a hidden passage or the like somewhere; we didn't want to lose the chance to find it.

"This doesn't feel right," I whispered.

"What do you mean? Is there something bothering you?" Rit replied.

Once I'd taken a moment to collect my thoughts, I answered, "After such a thorough search revealed nothing, I have to assume there's a concealed passage. But why did the ancient elves need to hide anything?"

"What do you mean?"

"When you have a room that you don't want people entering, what do you do, Rit?"

"What do…? Ah. I lock the door."

"Right. A hidden passage is only for special situations: when you don't want others to find something. For example, an escape route from a castle or a mage's secret research lab."

"Doesn't this place fit that description? The ancient elves were strange, and this is a deep underground structure."

"The ancient elves are hard to understand, but I think this place served a specific purpose. A practical facility has no use for a hidden door. That isn't really like them."

"Not like them, huh?" Rit racked her brain a bit.

"I can understand what you are getting at," Esta said. "But what do we do with that information?"

"I think we conclude that the ancient elves aren't the ones who hid the way forward. It was the wood elves who found this place later."

And knowing that told me where we needed to look.

✻　　　✻　　　✻

We all returned to that conspicuous wood elf sign.

"I brought it like you asked. What should we do with it?"

Danan set the body of a clockwork soldier that Ruti had defeated on the ground. This one was in comparatively better shape than the rest.

"There's something I wanted to try. I'm not sure it'll work, though, so don't get your hopes up," I explained with a wry smile. Rit and Van in particular watched me expectantly.

This could be embarrassing if nothing happens...

Fifteen minutes passed.

"Something's coming," Rit warned.

"Everyone, prepare to fight but don't move into position yet."

The whole group nodded and watched without drawing their weapons. Finally, I heard clacking footsteps.

"Ah!" Rit gasped in surprise.

There was a sound of gears as a four-legged clockwork golem appeared from a wall. A ripple ran across the metal wall where it emerged.

"This is...a wood elf spell!" I exclaimed.

"Like Loggervia's bewitching woods...!" Rit added.

It was powerful illusion magic that affected the mind. Dispelling it with modern magic was incredibly difficult.

"It influenced our minds to make us think there was a wall here. Because it's so powerful, even touching the disguised space feels like touching a wall. If you try to throw something at it, you'll unconsciously aim at the floor instead."

We'd seen earlier that parts from destroyed clockwork golems had been carried away, yet we couldn't determine where another of its kind would have gone were it responsible. The only answer was a secret passage we'd missed. Meaning there was a corridor the constructs could access that we couldn't. And if the wood elves, not the ancient elves, hid that route...

We were different from lifeless clockwork golems. A spell was likely manipulating our perception. That being the case, all we needed to do was rely on the clockwork golems.

"I see. I didn't notice at all," Yarandrala said as she carefully touched the wall. "Yeah, I still feel some resistance, but now that I know it is an illusion, I should be able to break through it."

The high elf Yarandrala knew a lot about wood elf magic. Even if completely dispelling it wasn't possible, we should be able to get by.

The clockwork golem that emerged picked up its fallen kin, turned back, and passed through the wall again, gears clacking all the while.

"Should we follow it?" Albert asked.

"Yeah, let's go. Is that fine with you, Van?"

"Of course!"

The Hero Administration Bureau awaited us.

What would we find?

*   *   *

We moved down the passage until coming to a door.

When the clockwork golem ahead of us approached, the door just slid open.

"Saves us the effort of forcing it."

We stepped through behind the clockwork golem. Inside, the room led to a big hall about six meters in radius.

"Looks like a lot of people came through here."

With a chamber this spacious, there must have been many ancient elves in this facility.

Farther down, there was a sizable gondola hanging from a rail that we could ride deeper into the facility.

"You know how to use that?" Danan asked.

I pointed at the clockwork golem.

"I'd guess that it does, so let's tag along."

"Oh, I get it. That's part of why you had me bring that busted construct along. Classic Red!"

I hadn't thought that far ahead at all. But in this sort of situation, it was better to act like you understood the whole time.

I grinned just a little bit, and Rit smirked at me.

She sees right through me...

*   *   *

The gondola moved along with a whir.

"This is going pretty far," Esta said.

True. We'd likely covered at least a kilometer already.

"How huge are these ruins?" Danan asked.

"It almost feels like they extend throughout the entirety of the area beneath the mountains," Albert responded.

Van and Lavender stared at the clockwork golem that was waiting, unmoving, at the edge of the gondola.

Rit and Yarandrala peered down the pitch-black passage and talked about the bewitching woods in Loggervia.

"The mood has improved," Esta remarked happily.

"It *has* been five days of dungeon crawling," I said.

"This is probably the first and last time the old and new Hero's parties will team up."

"Yeah."

"It was short, but I'm glad we were able to adventure together. I'm sure the members of my group learned a lot."

"Don't get ahead of yourself. Your real adventure is just beginning."

"Certainly. But we were in a really bad place, so seeing the party come together like this, I can't help but feel a bit…you know."

"It must have been rough for you."

"It will have been worthwhile if it leads to something."

I hadn't heard much more than a few vague snippets about what traveling with Van was like before. I assumed it was pretty grueling.

That Esta could say it was worth the trouble was enough for me to believe she was worthy of being called a hero herself.

✻ ✻ ✻

A room and passage waited at the other end of the gondola ride.

I pointed to the four-legged clockwork golem.

"I think it's about time to say good-bye to our friend and resume our search."

The construct was starting to move into another room with a hole resembling a trash disposal chute. The clockwork golem dropped the broken one it had picked up into the shaft, entered a box on the wall, and stopped moving.

"Let's save jumping down that chute for last," I said.

Van nodded. "I agree."

* * *

There were lots of devices in the ancient elf ruins. Most were too esoteric to divine their purposes, but I did spot something recognizable.

"Another wood elf sign."

It wasn't that surprising. They'd investigated this place, so it made sense that we found another sign.

"I'm glad there's no other spells hangin' around," Danan said with distaste.

That sort of problem was outside his specialty. He really couldn't handle tricky magic at all. A wood elf spell that he couldn't solve by fighting was his ultimate enemy.

"Well, I might not be able to win against a crazy illusion right now, but someday, I'll be able to punch through them."

"That's a little too muscle-brained…"

Despite my remark, Danan had managed to learn how to break locks and traps by punching them. When peace returned to the continent, he could establish a pretty popular school if he taught adventurers how to search dungeons using only their fists.

I decided to have a look at the wood elf sign.

"Hmm. What's this?"

Wood elves typically preferred overly long passages, yet this writing was quite brief.

"Past this point. The Hero's Calamity. Turn back…"

It was simple enough to decipher, but it didn't give us much to go on. Was that really all the wood elves wanted a reader to know?

"The Hero's Calamity?" Van asked.

He inspected the wood elf sign, confused.

"Yarandrala," I called.

"What?"

"Could you check to see if any wood elf spells are nearby?"

"Got it."

"You too, Lavender," I added.

"Huh? Me?" She looked entirely uninterested.

"Consider it a request from me, please."

"If you're asking, then leave it to me, Van!"

Yarandrala and Lavender both got to searching.

"It's safe. There are no spells placed here," Yarandrala concluded.

Lavender immediately flew back to Van's shoulder when she was finished. "Nothing! I worked hard, Van!"

I nodded, satisfied. "If Yarandrala and Lavender couldn't find anything, then I guess it's safe."

Wood elf magic could be dangerous because it was impossible to know the possible effects. Stumbling ignorant into spells was perilous.

However, if a high elf expert and a fairy who sensed magic by feeling didn't locate anything amiss, then we were okay.

"What is this 'calamity' it refers to?" Esta spoke with her voice tensed. The Hero was very important to her, so I could imagine this sign troubled her.

We fell into marching order and moved for the so-called Hero's Calamity.

✽ ✽ ✽

The phrase *The Hero's Calamity* brought to mind a few dangers.

My first thought was a facility that captured the Hero and performed cruel experiments. Perhaps the ancient elves were wiped out for transgressions against Demis. If so, then maybe they'd tried to analyze the Hero's power instead of allowing them to fulfill their role.

Admittedly, that was a very fanciful notion, but we were in ancient elf ruins. We walked among the remnants of a lost species that even the wood elves, whose technology and culture stood far beyond humanity's, viewed with fear and awe.

It wasn't inconceivable that a group might seek to obtain the Hero for their use. The Hero was stronger than an army, so taking them by force wasn't possible in the present day. However, the ancient elves could have developed weapons capable of surpassing the Divine Blessing. Maybe it was possible for them to overpower the Hero and force them to obey.

Thankfully, the surroundings didn't suggest such a danger yet.

We walked down a broad hallway. Occasionally, we passed doors on the left side of the corridor. We forced them open to reveal what looked like break rooms. There were remnants of beds and chairs.

"There sure are a lot of these rest chambers," I remarked.

Many ancient elves had worked at this facility.

"Seeing traces of activity from a race that disappeared thousands and thousands of years ago is kind of strange," Rit commented as she touched an uncomfortable-looking chair.

"I guess the cushioned part rotted away. Or maybe the ancient elves had really sturdy bottoms and preferred hard chairs," I said.

"Heh-heh, that's certainly an explanation. Do you know the answer, Lavender?"

"They were basically the same as you. I can't really tell the difference between them and you guys."

Lavender, the only one of us who'd seen ancient elves, shrugged with clear disinterest.

The hall turned to the left farther down. A large door marked the end of the passageway.

"Ah, a treasure chest!" Albert pointed to a box on the left wall with a shout.

It looked almost like a storage container, standing about two meters tall with a lock on the door.

Albert was an adventurer, so he naturally got excited about finding a treasure chest inside a dungeon.

"It is!"

"Let's open it and take a look inside!"

Rit and Yarandrala, who were also adventurers, sounded excited, too.

"...?"

Van looked puzzled. I guess that made sense. He'd never experienced a proper adventure and known the thrill of possibly striking it rich.

"What does your party do when you have to unlock something like this?" I said to him.

"I just ask Lavender."

Lavender puffed out her little chest when Van spoke her name.

"Oh? Then I would love to see you work," I remarked.

"Ha-ha-ha! A lock like this is nothing." Lavender flew over to the storage container.

"Ancient elf locks are enchanted with some unknown magic to only open with their matching key. Even master thieves struggle with them," I stated.

"Ha! Don't compare me to the likes of you!" Lavender conjured a seal before her hand. "Spirits, my words are your command. Open this lock."

There was a *click*, and the lock came undone.

Lavender flew up to my face and threw me a smug grin.

"That isn't fair," I said.

She'd cheated.

Lavender had used her massive presence to control the spirits. That had nothing to do with practice, knowledge, or skills provided by a blessing. It was merely a brute-force method that relied on her being an archfay of calamity.

"Thank you, Lavender. I'm glad you're in our party!" Van praised.

"Fu-fu-fu, if it makes you happy, I'll handle any lock!"

She really was helpful.

"Let's see what's inside." Rit urged me on.

Chapter 2: Dungeon Crawl

"Sure."

I opened the ancient elf container.

"These are…ancient elf weapons?!"

There were twelve-meter-long spears lined up neatly. But they presumably weren't ordinary armaments. If they were loaded with ancient elf magic, they could deploy a barrage like a massive crossbow and fire powerful energy blasts…supposedly.

That's what was written in the records of the royal library back at the capital.

"I…don't know how to use these," I muttered.

As spears went, they were light and short. I couldn't judge their sturdiness, but their ends weren't especially sharp. Without ancient elf magic, they were basically useless.

I looked to Van. "These will be worth a lot, and if you can figure out how to use them, they might be powerful weapons for soldiers. You should take them with you if you can put them in your item box."

"What? Are you sure it's fine for me to take all of them?"

I glanced at Danan and Yarandrala. They nodded.

"Yeah, they might be useful for you on your journey," I said.

Van seemed doubtful. "But they're valuable, right? None of us can wield them, and your shop could use some extra funds…"

"Hey."

Van had relaxed somewhat, but he could still be uptight.

"My shop is doing well enough for me to enjoy a pleasant life."

"Really?"

"Just take them already," I said. "Esta, put them in your item box."

I didn't want to get into a prolonged back-and-forth, so I turned to Esta for some help. She gazed ahead as though lost in thought.

"I see," she whispered. Had she noticed something?

"What is it?" Van asked.

"I was considering why there are weapons kept here. It feels odd to come across a box of them at the end of this passage so deep inside the ruins."

She had a point. That was curious.

Esta took one of the ancient elf spears and pointed it at the big door at the end of the hall.

"It's easy enough to aim at any target that came from that direction."

"Aim?"

"Should anything come storming through the door, picking them off from this distance would be a simple matter."

I imagined monsters surging from the entrance. I could picture the swarm of ogrekin we'd fought a little while back bursting out.

A one-sided barrage from here would solve that issue quickly.

"But that door leads deeper into the structure. I can understand repelling an attack from the opposite direction, but why would they prepare for one from within?"

Esta just shrugged at my question.

"I merely considered it from a strategic perspective. The answer to your query presumably lies ahead."

"Right. Let's go."

We'd find out more if we opened that large door.

With any luck, it would lead us to an answer about the nature of the Hero.

※　　　　　　※　　　　　　※

After breaking the lock, we forced the door open.

The passage continued, this time flanked by doors on both sides. The hall widened significantly here. If we got into a fight, there would be no worry of our weapons catching on the walls.

I perked up. "Oh, I never taught you how to fight with a sword in confined spaces, Van. Maybe we should address that tonight."

"How to fight in tight quarters? I can't wait."

"Ugh, nights are for me. You're cutting into my alone time with Van."

Van was excited, but Lavender was less than pleased.

The two of them had been such terrifying enemies, but now they were almost endearing.

"What is this...?" Rit said. As the party's scout, she'd been dutifully examining the doors and opened one.

"Something wrong?"

"Red...come here."

Rit looked stunned.

"Van, Lavender, let's go."

"Mhm."

We entered the room together.

"This is..." A quick look around left me at a loss for words, too.

There was a wall in front of us made of something like glass. The problem was the other side.

It was like a giant aquarium, but the liquid was definitely not water, and there weren't any fish. It was a thick, viscous, milky-white substance. Monsters floated inside. Dozens of chimeras...

"Corpses?" Esta asked as she took a few steps toward the tank.

Danan shook his head. "No, they're alive."

"You can tell?"

"Yeah. It's probably a suspended animation sort of thing. They're definitely alive, though. I can feel their vital force."

I guessed that was something provided by his Martial Artist blessing.

But if they're still alive...

"At best, these ruins are thousands of years old. To survive after all that time... Did the ancient elves discover the secret to eternal youth?" I said.

"I don't think the answer's quite that pleasant." There was sadness in Rit's eyes as she stared into the tank. "They are just being preserved so they don't die. They aren't really alive."

"Not really alive...," I echoed.

Rit loved freedom; she couldn't accept that any creatures, even monsters, were forced to suffer such an existence. She was clearly fighting back the urge to break the tank, but ultimately, she shook her head.

"What's all this for, then?" Van's question pulled us back from our astonishment.

What *was* this for?

A chimera preservation tank inside the Hero Administration Bureau.

I really don't like where this is heading.

"Ah, there's a trapdoor in the floor here... It looks like it continues down," Albert said after investigating the chamber.

There was a hatch set into the floor. I saw no means to release it save for a small hole. If we inserted a handle and spun it, the way would presumably open.

"Shall we search for the handle?" I suggested.

"That's too much work!" Lavender flew down from Van's shoulder and aimed her hands at the trapdoor. Then she squeezed the air. A small whirlwind funneled into the hole. She was manipulating air to turn the contraption.

That's a seriously handy ability.

"Mrgh," the fairy grunted.

Unfortunately, the door refused to yield. Lavender grimaced with evident annoyance.

I hummed. "Looks like it's locked tight. Finding the handle might not be enough."

Perhaps we'd come across a key if we searched the room.

"Like I said, that's too much work!" Lavender formed a seal with her left hand. "Spirits, my words are your command. Open this lock."

There was a loud *click*, and the lock spun as the door opened. There was a ladder descending downward on the other side of the door.

Got a taste for seeing me surprised last time? Well, fine, I'll indulge you.

"Wow, amazing," I said.

She kicked me right on the nose. That actually hurt.

"You're really amazing, Lavender."

"Thank you, Van!"

Not caring about me anymore after the kick, Lavender flew over to Van when he complimented her.

Sheesh.

ZAZAZA!

A grating noise sounded through the room.

"An alarm trap?!" I exclaimed.

"Impossible. The traps of mortals can't possibly catch me!" Lavender denied that possibility with the sort of arrogance befitting an archfay.

Hmm... This is...

"I think this is more like a Send Message spell than a trap."

"Send Message is for communicating with a distant target, right?" Van asked.

"Yeah." I nodded. "That noise resembled what happens when an amateur mage fails to cast Send Message."

Van cocked his head. "Really? I don't understand."

"There's a rhythm to it."

"A rhythm?"

"There's a bounce to the noise that feels like words. That was probably an ancient elf voice."

"An ancient elf voice!" Rit shouted. "So an ancient elf mage created a Send Message rune and engraved it to make it perpetual, but the rune's been worn away, so it could only produce a scrambled noise."

"The actual mechanics of it are probably a bit different, but that's likely close," I replied.

The grating noise continued. We were the audience to words from a species that went extinct thousands of years ago. Unfortunately, we couldn't understand any of it.

"Sounds like it really is just a trap," Danan remarked.

"I already told you it isn't!" Lavender fired back.

Hmm...

"Maybe the spirits undid some other lock, too?" I suggested.

"What do you mean?" Danan asked.

"Lavender opened the door by commanding spirits." It was a little hard to explain, but Lavender hadn't created a key. She'd demanded spirits to manipulate the lock to push it into an open position. "Maybe she undid something else that was connected to the door."

"Hmm," Danan murmured. "I only vaguely get it, but that's pretty nifty."

"Mhm!"

I'm not sure whether it was really all that amazing to unlock something you didn't mean to, but Danan's compliment seemed to improve Lavander's mood. That was good enough.

* * *

The ladder led to a massive, empty chamber. A sturdy door stood near the ladder, with another on the opposite side of the room.

Ancient elf script adorned both of them.

"This one is 'Exit,' and that one is 'Danger,'" I said.

The ancient elf language was almost entirely indecipherable, but those words were common enough that capable scholars had translated them.

"So it's dangerous?" Just as Rit put her hand on the hilt of her shotel...

Thump.

...Van, the last person climbing the ladder, reached the bottom.

"It looks almost like an arena."

No sooner had he said as much than another loud grating sound echoed.

"What?!"

We all immediately drew our weapons and got into fighting formation. The grating continued, issuing from the far wall.

This is...!

"Something's coming!" Rit shouted.

The door with *Danger* written on it opened, and a chimera leaped out.

"What, just a single chimera?" Van kept on guard, but he did sound surprised by the lack of a genuine threat.

No, that's...!

"That chimera's unusual!" I shouted.

"Huh?!" Van exclaimed.

"It has multiple blessings! Don't treat it like a normal one!"

The air around the chimera shimmered with heat. A moment later, a mass of flame came flying for us.

"Fireball?!" Esta exclaimed. The burning sphere landed in the middle of our group and exploded. Fortunately, we'd all scattered to safety. "That was a surprise, but the spell is less than what Sir Ares could manage!"

Esta leaped forward. Her left hand worked a spell to defend against any magical counterattack.

"Hahhh!!!"

Esta thrust her spear forward, but the chimera's massive body spun backward, evading her thrust.

"That was a Martial Artist skill!" I shouted.

The chimera stood on its hind legs and formed seals with its forelegs.

"Is that a Sage's Successive Activation?!" Esta cried, astonished.

"No! It's using Sorcerer and Adept blessings at the same time!" I replied.

A Dispel Magic spell erased Esta's defensive cast, and the chimera's second seal launched another Fireball.

"Crafty!" Esta was one of humanity's greatest clerical magic users. The chimera's Dispel Magic was insufficient to break her defensive spell. The Fireball's explosion swallowed her up, but she didn't suffer a single burn.

"An excellent feint, Lady Esta!" Albert praised.

The chimera leaped into the flames to land before Esta, swiping with its claws.

Martial Art: Swallow's Approach.

Apparently, the monster had access to skills from the Warrior tree. Van and I closed in to deliver mortal blows.

"You're right. Swallow's Approach really is full of openings once you understand how it works."

"Right?"

Van's sword thrust up through the chimera's neck as my blade slashed through its spine from above. The chimera's massive body slumped to the ground before it could complete its attack.

"All right," I said.

It wasn't a difficult battle, but it put up some resistance. That was more than could be said of most monsters when paired against our party.

I stowed my sword.

"Ah."

It had been so long since I felt this sensation that I audibly gasped.

"What is it, Red?" asked Rit.

"My level went up."

The last time my blessing level increased was back while I was traveling with Ruti. It had never increased during my time in Zoltan.

Closing my eyes, I could sense the ability to develop one of my skills when I connected with my blessing.

"Congrats!" Rit said.

"Thanks. When we get back, maybe I'll put it into my Cooking skill."

I smiled at her.

And here I thought my level was never going to go up again...

The celebration was cut short as the grating sound filled the room again.

"What?"

We all readied ourselves.

"Another one!" Rit shouted.

A chimera just like the last one appeared through the open door.

"Everyone, spread out!" I commanded. "It has a wide variety of offensive options, but each one is from a low-tier blessing. Don't panic, and you should be fine!"

"Obviously!" Danan wore a savage expression as he jumped forward. "You got out in front of me last time, but I damn sure want to fight a Martial Artist chimera!"

"Me too!" Rit went with him.

The chimera fired off magic at the approaching enemies.

※ ※ ※

"Arrrrgh! It never ends!" Rit's sword tore into a chimera's stomach, then Esta's spear ran the monster through when it staggered.

"This is the ninth one." After making sure it was dead, Esta paused to catch her breath.

Everyone still had plenty of strength to spare. However, we were concerned this would keep going, adding extra stress.

"There's no end to it... Should we retreat?" Albert asked.

Albert's blessing level had already risen three times. His level was notably lower than everyone else's, but the amount he'd grown from the stream of chimeras was unreasonable.

"But we can't just leave chimeras that can use magic and Martial Arts here. It would be a problem if they started rampaging through the ruins."

Esta faced the door and readied her spear again.

"But that tank upstairs had a lottt of chimeras in it," Lavender reminded.

What do we do?

"Red!" Van dashed forward. "We will fight the chimeras! You focus on thinking of a way out of this situation, please!"

"That's the spirit, Van." A small, pleased smile crossed Esta's lips. "Leave this to the new Hero's party."

"Got it!"

They engaged the tenth chimera to keep my group safe while we handled the other issue.

"What caused the chimeras to start appearing?" Rit asked.

Rit raised her sword to protect me, and her eyes trained on the chimera.

The cause...

"They've gotta be coming from that tank upstairs, right? Why don't we smash it?" Danan glared up at the ceiling.

He was almost definitely right. That was likely the source.

"That's probably not a good idea," I replied. "If the monsters came alive at once, things could get bad."

"Not if we beat them all. But fine, we'll save that as a last resort. If it comes to that, you can leave it to me!"

"Ha-ha, I'll be counting on you."

Danan's comments helped lighten the mood.

I don't think he was aiming for that when he said it, but it reminded me how crucial he was to the party.

I returned my attention to the cause of our predicament.

Why did the chimeras appear?

The system activated when we entered the room. In particular, it started the moment Van set foot here. But why? The odds of a trap were low. A trap would have a more direct method of killing us. There was no need for such a massive setup. Clockwork golems could have dealt with intruders.

"Is this intended to increase the Hero's level?" I wondered aloud. That would explain why it had to be chimeras and not constructs. The former were alive, meaning they possessed Divine Blessings like every other living creature. Divine Blessings grew by killing beings who possessed Divine Blessings. The chimeras didn't have multiple blessings to make them stronger. It was because killing one of them was akin to defeating multiple monsters, making for an efficient way to level up.

Van had killed the tenth chimera and was fighting the eleventh. This battle would make his blessing grow.

"Don't get distracted," I chided myself.

Strictly speaking, the system didn't activate when we entered the room. A mechanism like that would be too dangerous. Lavender undoing the door lock had likely started this. It must have released a seal on this system. How would we stop it?

"Lavender! Use the spirits to lock the door leading up!" I called.

"Huh?!"

"Please! That should stop the chimeras!"

"If you're wrong, I'll never let you live it down!"

Lavender fired off a bolt of lightning magic at the chimera before flying for the door.

"Spirits, my words are your command. Close this lock."

Click. The grating sounded once more. The rhythm was different this time, though. It was nerve-racking. A warning, perhaps?

"...Right! Everyone, get away from the chimera!" I called.

Van and his party quickly moved back. No sooner did they do so than a swell of magic flowed from the walls.

"What's going on, Red?!"

"If this is a room for raising one's blessing level, then it has to have a system for dealing with the monsters, too."

The system had started in response to Lavender opening the way. So closing the hatch would stop the process. And considering that the ancient elves were thorough enough to create a structure that operated long after they went extinct, they would have a procedure in place for dealing with leftover monsters.

The magic power emanating from the walls formed a magic circle in midair.

A shaft of light pierced the chimera.

Ker-clunk!

After an odd noise, the magic that illuminated the chamber dissipated.

"Huh?"

The chimera was still alive. In fact, it looked undamaged.

"Lightning Speed!"

Using my skill, I approached the monster in a flash, finishing it off while it was still wobbly from the light.

The grating sound died out. There was no sign of another chimera coming.

We did it!

"That's my Red!" Despite Rit's compliment, I felt a bit embarrassed that my prediction had been slightly off. "We need to see, too. Light."

Rit's spell illuminated the surroundings with her magic. Lavender, who was over by Van, had used a similar spell. I pulled a light stick out from my pouch, hit it against the floor to get it shining, and put it into my belt.

"That was a crazy trap," Danan said.

"No, I don't think it was a trap," I replied.

"What do you mean?"

I told everyone my theory about this being a room for empowering the Hero.

Van looked shocked. "So all those monsters in that tank are for the Hero?"

During the battle, Rit, Yarandrala, Van, Albert, and I all leveled up. Such efficiency was impossible with normal fighting.

"I bet the ogrekin that Rit and I fought earlier recently escaped from this complex. It was probably for a lower-level Hero."

The chimeras that inhabited the area around the ruins were likely descendants of those that had escaped the facility. None of them had multiple blessings, though. Maybe the technology could grant an individual creature multiple blessings, but not its offspring.

Divine Blessings were bequeathed by God. All living beings had one. No one could complain about a gift from Demis or seek to defy it. That's what the church taught anyway. The ancient elves had broken that tenet.

I looked at Van. He'd also received an extra blessing in a way. And the Devil's Blessing given by the contract demon did something similar. The ability to manipulate blessings was beyond human knowledge, yet it was clearly possible.

Plenty of people were unsatisfied with their blessings. And many took umbrage with having their future limited at birth.

Would humans someday develop the technology to manipulate blessings like the ancient elves?

I recalled Lavender's comment about how they were no different from us.

"I see. So it's like a colosseum," Danan said as he examined a chimera corpse lying on the ground. "Running around catching monsters is a hassle, and there aren't many that can reliably raise our blessing levels."

"True. In that sense, I guess the intent does resemble a colosseum."

Most cities on the continent had a fighting arena of some kind. Part of the goal was the entertainment of seeing warriors clash with each other, but the main goal was to create a setting to raise people's levels safely. People could fight captured monsters in an environment with help ready and able if things went wrong.

Audiences enjoyed watching others fight to grow their blessings, so it became entertainment. Ultimately, colosseum matches became a show where humans could face each other in contests of skill.

It was expensive to go out and catch monsters, so to cover that expense, tickets were sold.

"There aren't any spectator seats, though." Rit sounded a little disappointed. "Did the ancient elves just not like arena matches?"

"Hard to say. Or maybe it is because this facility was specifically for the Hero."

Rit had joined the colosseum for fun back when she was an adventurer in Loggervia. She had even challenged Ruti to a fight in the colosseum to make her look bad...though Rit ended up losing.

Ruti was the wrong person to challenge.

"So the Hero Administration Bureau was a facility for training the Hero, then?" Van asked after thinking for a while.

"It seems like that was part of its role, at least," I replied.

"You think there was more to it?"

"Yeah. If it was just a training facility, creating such a massive place would be unnecessary. I imagine there's another purpose."

"So there's more to the Hero's secret."

"All we know is that this institution is for the Hero. There's got to be more to why the wood elves left that warning."

We had to keep going.

"No light makes this place very inconvenient to navigate," Yarandrala said as she cast her own illumination magic.

Blessings that can use magic sure are convenient.

"I'll make some light, too," Danan said.

I blinked. "Wait, what?"

Danan smirked and started breathing in a particular way. His body began to shine.

"The skill's called Fire Snake's Breathing. How's that?"

It was a super-high-level skill involving chi movement. Fire Snake's Breathing allowed the user to breathe underwater or jump in midair. It was my first time seeing it. Apparently, it made the body glow.

"The Divine Blessing of the Martial Artist has some handy stuff," I remarked. How unfair that everyone else had useful abilities.

I glanced over at Albert. He smiled wryly.

"I can't make any light, either," he said. "Still though, why did it suddenly go dark?"

"The ruins likely ran out of power," I replied.

"Ran out of power?"

"I think we'll find out why if we investigate more. Either way, we should leave this room for now."

"Right...which way should we take out?" Albert motioned to the hatch at the top of the ladder and then to the door marked with the ancient elf word for *Exit*. Ignoring the door with *Danger* written on it was probably best.

"The hatch overhead is locked... Considering the construction of this place, I think the door we took down was more for emergency use. This one should take us back," I said.

"All right, then let's check it out." Rit moved over to the door. "Huh? It isn't locked."

It yielded when she pushed.

"That looks heavy. I'll help."

"Me too."

With me and Albert pushing, as well, the door opened quickly.

"I thought it would be locked in order to keep the chimeras from getting out. That's strange." Rit cocked her head.

She was right. It was a little odd…

"Maybe it was sealed using magic and unlocked now that the power is gone," I suggested.

"What? That sounds so careless."

"Well, it's open, so let's not question our good fortune."

Chapter 3
Please Believe in My Love

What was the Hero?

Why did Divine Blessings exist? What was Demis's goal in creating Divine Blessings? Why did God create this world at all?

The ancient elves could manipulate Divine Blessings, and thus, they knew the answers to those questions.

The Hero blessing burdened a single person with the fate of the entire world. What possible reason was there for such an unreasonable destiny?

I couldn't begin to imagine the number of lives that had come and gone during this world's millions of years of existence, but they all had their own stories. And yet the story of a single person picked out from the rest in the world determined the fate of every other tale.

From a human's perspective, the Hero could easily seem like a martyr for the rest of the world. But from God's perspective, perhaps the world was a stage all for the Hero.

When I was studying the Hero blessing to help Ruti, I thought I wanted to know the answer to that question. But after choosing to live a simple, slow life, I realized I no longer needed that information.

And that was still true. Without the Hero, the demon lord across the sea would likely continue living. However, the forces of Avalon were still pushing the demon lord's army back. Kingdoms were strong enough to protect their lands. That was enough to end the war.

Someday in the future, humans might advance in the art of shipbuilding, and that could lead to a larger conflict. Perhaps that would lead to the demon lord's downfall. Regardless, it was a story for the future.

Wasn't it enough to protect our families here and now?

*   *   *

There was a clicking sound.

"The lights are back," I muttered.

They flickered to life in the hallway.

"It feels like this place is on its last legs…"

We'd made a lot of progress in our exploration.

There had been dozens of abandoned structures. More than half of the tanks filled with monsters were destroyed, and their inhabitants were dead. Some looked like they'd been smashed long ago, but most of the damage appeared recent, judging by the decay—no more than a few months.

Had something occurred here not long ago that shortened the facility's life span?

Undoubtedly, it had to do with Ruti and the Asura demon Shisandan breaking into the ruins.

"A lot of the magic power stored here has seemingly been exhausted," I said.

"That's why the system to kill the chimera didn't properly activate," Rit replied.

"That magic weapon fired off a massive amount of magic power. It ran out partway and made the entire facility stop functioning."

"But then why did the lights come back on?" Rit asked.

"I'd guess that when the magic power gets low, lesser systems are abandoned for more important ones."

"Like a lizard sacrificing its own tail."

"Yeah, almost like it's a living organism."

The people who built this compound died long ago, yet the structure itself persisted, sacrificing parts of itself to keep going. Even though there was no one left to use it.

No, that's not true. We're learning a lot because it managed to survive all this time. It's lived on to teach someone about those who made it...

I mulled over the idea while we walked.

*   *   *

"It looks like we are almost at the end," I said when we reached a sturdy door.

"How do you know?" Van asked, curious.

"Instinct."

"Instinct... Is that reliable?"

"More than you'd think."

I had explored countless dungeons. Those experiences had given me an idea of how dungeons were typically constructed, and that granted me the insight to predict what might lie ahead.

"Most of your adventures have been for raising your level, but you'll gain the same feeling in time," I assured him.

"You think so?" Van looked doubtful.

I wonder how Ruti would feel?

She'd been everywhere, too. Did she have the same kind of instinct?

Perhaps we could all visit some safe, fully explored ruins for a bit of sightseeing one day. Sharing stories about old dungeons while walking around sounded like fun.

That would have to wait, though. We needed to deal with the door.

"Rit, please."

"Leave it to me." Rit approached the door and examined it. "It's locked. It looks more complex than the ones before, but I'll see if I can force it."

After a little bit of time...

"Argh! There's no way! It doesn't feel like this door was even made to be opened!" ...Rit threw her hands up in frustration.

"Should we leave it to Lavender?" I suggested.

"Yeah, I'm out of tricks." Rit looked over at Lavender, who was sitting on Van's shoulder. He nodded and asked the fairy, "Could you?"

"Of course! Anything for you!"

Lavender was in a great mood. She cheerfully called upon the spirits.

"Wait," Esta said, hurrying up to Van. "If Lavender does it her way, something unexpected might happen again."

Click.

All of a sudden, the door began to shudder. A massive amount of dust fell to the floor as it opened.

This seemed like more than a simple door. It was a complex mechanism made up of several parts that each unlocked in turn.

What elaborate construction... No wonder Rit couldn't do anything with it.

"It opened," Esta remarked.

"It did," Van agreed.

They both looked surprised.

"Esta, something on you is shining," Van said.

"What?" Esta pulled out the proof of the Hero, which was faintly glowing, from a pocket beneath her armor.

"Is the proof of the Hero reacting to something?" I asked.

"It looks like that is the key to this door," Esta replied.

A key? Was this complex linked to the Hero's ruins near the capital?

"Only the Hero can obtain this item. Which means the area ahead is reserved for the Hero," Esta remarked.

Rit nodded. "So the ruins where the proof of the Hero was found had to be cleared first."

The two women seemed to agree. Was that all there was to this, though?

It made sense if God had made these ruins, but the ancient elves built these halls. Why would they make a section only accessible to the Hero?

The proof of the Hero was an item that enhanced the Hero's blessing. Maybe we just never considered its actual purpose because its power was linked to the Hero, and only the Hero could obtain it. Perhaps the answer was simple: It was a difficult key to reproduce.

I had no way of knowing, but one thing was for sure.

"Demis and the ancient elves had very different goals."

What did the ancient elves see in the Divine Blessing of the Hero?

Presumably, there were more systems for the Hero in the ruins. Most of them had stopped functioning after ages of no use, and we'd walked past others because we couldn't discern their purposes with our limited knowledge.

There was no way we could skip what we found here, though.

"Another Holy Demon Slayer..."

The path beyond the door split to the left and right. There was another door at the end of both routes. We were in the room beyond the door at the end of the left way.

This chamber was, to put it simply, the Hero's armory.

"Twenty-four Holy Demon Slayers, eleven proofs of the Hero, and lots of armor, helmets, and shields that were likely for the Hero," I remarked.

Legendary equipment lined the place as though it were a shop.

If a cleric of the church saw this, they'd faint on the spot.

I glanced at Esta.

"I see...," she muttered, approaching one of the sacred swords and picking it up.

"Are you all right?"

"Red, if you were God, and you wanted to defeat the demon lord..." Instead of answering, she asked me a question. Entertaining the idea of someone else being God was pretty taboo, yet it didn't seem to trouble Esta. "...What would be the most efficient way to give people sacred weapons to achieve that goal?"

"Hmm. I'd probably spread them among all of the Hero's party. Or maybe teach people how to make them for themselves."

"Yet that isn't what Demis did. God's machinations are beyond mortal comprehension." Esta nodded as she looked at the blade. "A fine sword. It's a match for the one that Ruti wielded."

"Esta."

"I don't know God's plan, but I do understand what the ancient elves thought. They were of the same mind as you, Red."

"You mean we can wield these?" I asked.

"Yes. The ancient elves took the Holy Demon Slayer—or more precisely, the Sacred Avenger that Shisandan used—modified it, and replicated it so anyone can wield it."

"An imitation sacred sword..."

"It's not that shocking. Taking the knowledge gained from a sacred sword meant for the Hero to create armaments for everyone else is a pretty reasonable notion." Esta put the sword back. "Mass-produced sacred blades and ancient elf magic spears. Both would be useful for slaying the demon lord."

"You look calm. I'm surprised."

"I've been thinking about God and Divine Blessings a lot recently. I believe I have some idea of what the Hero meant to the ancient elves." There was confidence in her words.

"What the Hero meant, huh?" I muttered.

"Just the answer the ancient elves reached," Esta reminded.

I didn't feel nearly so confident. After thinking about it for a while, I noticed Van approaching the swords with a deep interest.

"So this is the Holy Demon Slayer...," Van whispered with reverence.

"Don't touch it!" I shouted on reflex. The boy looked at me in surprise.

"Sorry for shouting. When Ruti held a sacred sword here, her blessing went berserk."

"What?!"

Shisandan's final plan had been to force Ruti to take the Sacred Avenger, causing the Hero blessing to overtake her consciousness. As a result, Ruti had tried to cut through Tisse and me because we were in the way of her fulfilling the Hero's duties.

It was a terrible memory for her.

"It's okay," Esta said as she picked up the sword. "These weapons don't have the power to make the Hero run wild."

She passed one of the swords to Van. He took it from her cautiously.

"…!"

There was a look of shock on his face.

"It's like power is welling up inside me! This is the holy blade that Demis gave the Hero to defeat the demon lord."

"It's a replica of that weapon," Esta corrected. "As you can see, it does not affect the Hero's impulses, even when Van touches it."

I brought a hand to my chin. "So the ancient elves removed that quality."

"Well, that aspect is quite the drawback," Esta replied frankly.

"Are you really okay, Esta? What have you figured out about these ruins?"

"I'm sure you'll realize it soon enough."

Van and I were confused by her response, but Esta was content to leave it at that. She addressed Van and the rest of the party with a little smile.

"All right. This is an armory stocked with the most powerful weapons and armor. Let's take as much as we need."

Van grabbed a holy blade and a full set of armor. Albert switched into equipment that Esta recommended. And Esta also picked up a sacred blade and hung it at her hip.

"This will do just fine as a backup if my spear ever breaks."

It was the sacred blade spoken of in legends of the Hero, even if it was just a copy fabricated by the ancient elves. Esta had distanced herself from the church, but she'd been raised as a cleric. To carry a sacred weapon as a spare should have been unthinkable.

Next was the final room.

* * *

Rit forced the lock on the last door, the entrance to the deepest corner of the Hero Administration Bureau.

Inside were three long desks lined up together. A mysterious orb floated in the air. Close inspection revealed it was a map of the world.

"The map is a little different, but I guess that's because it's thousands of years old...or maybe our maps just aren't that precise. Amazing." I moved closer to the orb.

When I touched it, the area I prodded with a finger floated up and expanded. It was like a magic-induced illusion. However, this one wasn't meant to conceal something or befuddle people, but to show greater detail.

It seemed like something that modern-day magic could replicate.

"All the last room has is an atlas?" Danan sounded a little disappointed. "I guess the secrets of the Hero ended with that armory."

"Hey, there's a black mark and characters written on the globe," I motioned to the spot in question.

Danan squinted. "Huh? That's where Zoltan is, right?"

Many black dots covered the map section that had expanded.

Danan and I were suspicious.

"So that's it." Peering closer, I realized what it was. "These are people."

"What do you mean?"

"Look, that big bunch of dots is a town, right?"

"Now that you mention it, yeah, it's gotta be."

"And we can enlarge the map again."

The globe's controls were intuitive. Touching the enlarged section created another section that was more zoomed in. Pushing in against the original expanded area closed it.

How convenient.

"This is incredible. You can see everyone moving around," I said.

The people came and went, moving along the streets. Some stopped

Chapter 3: Please Believe in My Love

at food stalls, others chatted near walls, and more talked in the church...

"With this, you could know the movements of every army in the world."

This globe solved almost every issue there was with commanding an army.

If you could carry it with you, your forces would be invincible. The globe seemed wasted below the ground in the middle of nowhere.

"Hey, what's this writing?" Van pointed at the map.

Small characters were lined up vertically next to the moving people.

"I wonder..." I took a careful look. "Hmm. I can read some of them..."

"You can?"

"As long as they're just single words. This one is probably 'Warrior.'"

I'd reviewed ancient elf documents about blessings before. Warrior was the most common blessing among ancient elves, just as it was with humans, followed by Fighter, Mage, and other lower-tier blessings. I still recalled how *Warrior* was written on that old document.

"So then this place has an Appraisal ability?!" Van cried in disbelief.

He had every reason to be surprised. Honestly, I was, too.

There were only two blessings capable of using Appraisal: Sage and Saint. But the ancient elves were able to replicate it via pure magic. No, it went beyond mere imitation. Casting Appraisal on every single person in the world was an absurd achievement.

"Ancient elves..." I felt like we were missing something very critical. The map only showed people's blessings. There were no monsters listed.

I zoomed in on the area around Zoltan, focusing down to the room we were in. There were six dots. Van was highlighted on the display, perhaps because the Hero was special. However, there were eight of us. Two were missing.

One was Lavender, since she was a fairy. Who was the other?

"Yarandrala's not marked."

The high elf Yarandrala was absent from the map.

This device only showed humans, so it followed that she was left out. But why only track humans?

"If the ancient elves made this globe, don't you think it's strange that it doesn't show elves?"

There were no records of how prosperous humanity was during the age of the ancient elves. However, humanity had struggled to survive in tribes several hundred years ago, during the era of the wood elves. I doubted that humans had powerful societies even further back in history. The prevailing theory posited that any humans living at that time were mere barbarians.

So why track human blessings?

Lavender was the only one among us who'd ever seen an ancient elf before, so I asked her.

"Lavender, please tell me something. Were ancient elves' ears more like mine or Yarandrala's?"

"Ears? Those annoying creatures had ones more like yours." Lavender pointed at my head.

"I see. So there never were any ancient elves."

To Lavender, there was hardly any difference at all between humans and elves. She'd never given much consideration to the meanings of the words. Ancient people or ancient elves, the difference was for others to concern themselves with, not her.

"Humans made these ruins," I said.

Esta seemed to realize something at that. "I see." Turning around, she examined an ancient elf device attached to the desk. "That makes it a lot easier to understand the point of this Hero Administration Bureau than if some mysterious extinct people had created it."

"The point..."

"Hmm, looks like I should be able to make it work."

"You know how to use it?"

"As a clerical magic user, I've studied many spells, although I really only understand one function. It helps that they made a display that anyone can use."

Esta moved the device using magic, and the globe changed.

"The points on the map moved," I commented.

At Esta's alteration, the dots representing people changed.

"Now there's no marks in this room... Oh! These are past records?" I said.

"Yes. This should be from one year ago," Esta replied.

"...Incredible. So we can view where people were in the past."

"You were still in Zoltan a year ago, correct?"

"Yeah. I hadn't opened the shop yet, but I was living in a town house." I shifted the map back to Zoltan and pointed to a single dot.

Esta pursed her lips. "If this is a record of the past, then let's see if my guess is right."

"Guess...?"

The points representing people started flickering violently. The number of black dots shrank. We were watching time rewind to the era of the wood elves. History was flowing backward at lightning speed.

Suddenly, the number of humans exploded.

"What's going on?! There are humans everywhere, even on the dark continent!" I cried.

"This is during the time when this facility was built...when humanity was in its golden age," Esta explained. She continued to operate the device. Time began to move more slowly for the globe.

"There," she said. "The Hero and the demon lord." There were two points highlighted on the map. "The demon lord wasn't a human, but they're highlighted because they're special, I guess."

"Probably," I agreed. "It makes sense, given the goal of this map."

Esta slowly moved backward through time.

"Back then, humans ruled the dark continent, too, so the demon lord was surrounded by the Hero and other warriors and immediately slain."

"It was over in an instant...," Van muttered.

"The demon lord was easily dealt with in that era," I said.

"Sounds like a good thing," Yarandrala remarked.

"Right, the demon lord couldn't hurt anyone," Rit agreed.

Van did not take this news as well as the others. "But then there's no reason for the Hero and the demon lord to exist!" he shouted.

Esta nodded.

"That's what the ancient humans concluded. Rather than trusting the Hero to complete God's trial, they created a situation where they would win every time. The Hero's mere existence doesn't change much. God made the Hero and the demon lord as the most important pieces on the board, but the battle was too important to risk. The people stole it away from the Hero."

Esta reversed the flow of time for the map. History marched forward in its natural course now. The Hero's short adventure began and ended quickly. After defeating the demon lord, the Hero returned to the Hero Administration Bureau here and remained inside.

Hmm... I see.

"If the Hero remained outside, their impulses would compel them to save others. This place is so deep and hidden because it's meant to sever the Hero from the outside world," I stated.

Esta nodded. "Yes. That's the same conclusion I came to."

So that's why she'd been brooding.

This was the solution to the Hero and demon lord problem that the ancient, advanced humans devised—this bureau. It was a facility dedicated to managing the Hero's life so they didn't have to quest or battle.

"That's... That's the Hero's life? I can't accept that!" Van shouted.

Van was driven to fulfill his role as the Hero by his religious faith. The Hero of the ancient human era was inconceivable to him.

"You don't have to accept it. It's merely how things were in the past." Esta's blunt remark seemed to shock Van.

The ancient humans understood and commandeered the Divine Blessing system God created.

"Once, I thought if God wished for the Hero to die for the world, then that was simply a necessary sacrifice." Esta stared at the dots representing a long-gone Hero and demon lord. "However, that would mean the Hero existed purely to be offered to stop a recurring phenomenon. That hardly seemed like the sort of person who'd inspire courage in others."

"...You're right. The ancient humans just chose the most effective and efficient method of limiting damage," I said.

"Indeed. The humans didn't make a mistake. Demis did." Esta, a cleric, was rejecting God's actions.

Everyone else in the room was floored, but I understood Esta's feelings.

"Demis clearly wanted something to come of the battle between the Hero and the demon lord, but it wasn't this pointless, repeated fighting. From the moment things turned out that way, Demis should have abandoned the Divine Blessing of the Hero altogether." I looked at Van. His eyes were fixed forlornly on the shifting map.

Lavender snuggled up to him, trying to warm his heart and break the chill that had settled over him.

"Van," I called.

"Red...what is the Hero's purpose? You said I would find an answer if I came here, but I feel all the more lost..."

"Ancient humans used the Hero as a method to quell the recurring disaster that was the birth of a new demon lord. It's a logical way of looking at it."

"I hate the idea of that kind of Hero!"

"But with a broader perspective, you could say that it does fulfill the blessing's role. There's no adventure and no drama to a battle that will never be lost, but it's still a fight against evil."

"It's wrong, though! My heart tells me that isn't heroic at all!"

I smiled and nodded. "Sounds like you have your answer, then."

"My...answer...?"

"You are the one who will decide the sort of hero you become. The hero you want to be, the life you want to live, the ending you want to reach. I think you should live as you please."

I wanted Van to know more about his blessing not because I wanted him to be a proper Hero, but because I wanted him to live his life for himself.

The Hero's impulses were powerful. The Divine Blessing would surely shackle him, and it would be difficult for him to live freely. Still, I didn't want him to give up on his life because of that. Even if he lived as his blessing demanded, I wanted it to be because he decided to.

"I don't understand...," Van muttered with his head lowered. After a moment, he raised it with a determined look. "But I want to travel, talk to Esta and Lavender and Ljubo, meet lots of other people, and discover the sort of hero I want to be."

"That's fine," Esta said. She and everyone else smiled at Van's answer. This moment was surely the true beginning of Van the Hero's journey.

"Lavender, do you hate Van now that he's like this?" I asked.

"I'll kill you for saying something so stupid. Van is always wonderful...but today, he's even better than usual!"

Lavender started to kiss Van's cheek...but then froze.

"What is it, Lavender?" I had a terrible feeling that something was wrong.

Lavender slowly turned her gaze toward the ceiling. She glared hard at it, as though looking through it.

"Don't you dare touch Van!!!" Lavender screamed as cracks appeared all over her small body.

Something in the sky seemed so threatening that her true nature emerged.

"Lavender?!" Rit shouted, but the fairy did not have the wherewithal to reply.

What's happening?!

Everyone was just as confused as me.

Van alone was different. His expression remained unchanged—frozen in a smile from the end of our conversation.

This is bad!

I drew my sword and ran over to Lavender.

"Ahhh." Lavender gasped. Her body was rigid. "Van..."

Misery colored her voice.

Van's sword had cut into her. Blood erupted, and she collapsed to the floor limply. Just as Van was about to deal the final blow, I grabbed

Chapter 3: Please Believe in My Love

Lavender's body and tried to escape the reach of his blade. Unfortunately, he was too fast.

He's quicker than Ruti!

"Kh!!!"

I raised my sword to meet the strike. It was the perfect defensive response, yet I was sent flying through the air by the force of the blow.

While tasting that special sort of uneasiness that came from being aloft, I readied myself for the landing.

Something slammed into my back.

I was flung all the way to the ceiling…?!

I bounced against the ceiling and dropped to the floor at high speed. There wasn't even a moment to activate my Acrobatics skill.

"Argh…!"

My body shuddered from the violent impact. That single attack was enough to incapacitate me. I couldn't stand.

"V-Van…"

I struggled to get that word out of my spasming lungs.

Van was smiling with the expression of a true believer, just like when he first came to Zoltan.

"Ahhh. The Lord has come. The Hero shall destroy evil and save the people. Because that is why the Hero exists." He spoke with feverish excitement.

Esta was next to react. "Has he gone berserk like Ruti?!"

When Ruti was ensnared by the holy blade because of Shisandan, her Hero blessing overtook her when she tried to abandon her role. It had dulled her senses and compelled her to eliminate us.

Had Van's blessing gone wild in the same way?

"N…no…"

I couldn't form words properly, but I had to warn them.

"Van! I'll heal you later, but I'll need to take a limb for now!"

"I'll help!"

Esta leaped forward to stop Van while Yarandrala conjured a seal to support her.

I had to stop them... They couldn't win against Van now... No one alive could.

"Red, are you okay?!" Rit rushed over to me to heal my wounds and Lavender's.

Esta and Yarandrala collapsed in the blink of an eye.

Two of the strongest people in the world were cut down in a single stroke.

"No..." Rit couldn't believe the terrible scene before her eyes. She stopped moving for just a moment.

Not good...!

"Ah?!" Rit exclaimed.

Van closed the distance immediately, turning his sword on Rit.

Emotion consumed me as I poured all my strength into my limbs in an attempt to stand. But I knew I couldn't make it in time.

A large shadow lunged for Van from a blind spot.

Danan!

He'd kept still until now because he understood instinctually that Van now possessed a terrifying level of power. Normally, he would've been the first to dive in, yet he hadn't flinched as Esta and Yarandrala fell. He'd been waiting for the right moment.

"Martial Art: Rising Dragon's Roar!!!"

Danan's full-powered attack...never got off the ground.

"S-sorry, Red..."

Van's sword moved far faster than Danan, piercing his body.

He was too strong. Even the ultimate Martial Artist couldn't do anything.

This was more than the Hero going berserk.

When she lost control, Ruti was weaker than usual. Because she couldn't wield a sword to her true capabilities when acting solely on impulses.

Van was different. His fighting style remained. However, his physical abilities, his reaction time, and his blessing's skills had all been enhanced to an impossible extent.

Chapter 3: Please Believe in My Love

The map that displayed blessings turned red. The point marking Van was highlighted. Next to it, written in the ancient script, was his blessing and level.

The Hero, Level 100.

It was a true miracle.
There was only one being who could possibly do something like that.
Van's Divine Blessing changing from the Cardinal to the Hero was already a miracle. Had he decided that another wouldn't hurt? Had he poured strength directly into Van's blessing to bring about one more act of providence?
The being who brought so much chaos to people's lives was here before me.
"Is that you, Demis?!" I demanded.
God was present, through Van.
"The Lord has come. I have awakened as a true hero... I am a savior."
Demis was speaking in Van's voice.
It was a farce. What true hero? What savior? Demis had merely inserted himself into his own creation to speak through a puppet's lips.
My head grew hot, and I trembled in rage.
Van had grown.
His transformed blessing had confused him, he'd made lots of mistakes, but he'd finally managed to find his own way. He'd discovered the hero he wished to be. He had tasted frustration after losing to me, learned the joy and fun of swordsmanship, and he could smile and laugh during adventures with his comrades.
He was finally ready to set off on his journey.
And this miracle overwrote all of it.
Demis was obliterating everything Van had gained, deeming it worthless.
"Bullshit..."

I was furious.

The absurdity of this development made me forget my pain. I stood and leveled my sword at God.

"Demis, you are the creator of this world. Van's body, Van's blessing, Van's soul—you made each. Maybe that's why you think you can do whatever you please with them." I glared at Demis. "But Van's resolve was born of himself! That doesn't belong to anyone else! That was his alone! Right?! Answer me, Demis!"

"No," Demis answered gently in Van's voice, as if patiently explaining to a child. "The bodies, the blessings, the will that God gave all of you are your own. God loves you."

"Love?"

The blood of Van's comrades dripped from the sacred sword Demis held loosely.

"You talk of love after cutting down Van's friends?"

"Be not sad. Flesh and spirit may perish, but souls are eternal. God's love is devoted to all of you. This world knows more of God's love and benevolence than any of the infinite others."

I'd always imagined what the deity who forced the Hero onto Ruti was like.

I didn't like Demis. You could say I held a grudge against him. However, I understood that God had his reasons for things and also that people wished for Demis to save them. The morals of society had been shaped through the lens of religion.

So even if I carried a grudge, I didn't hate him.

Until now!

"This isn't the first time you've deigned to come down here, is it?" I pressed him. "When the world fell out of line from what you desired, you intervened and created another Hero…and you were the one who destroyed the ancient humans' civilization."

Demis was the reason for the differences between Ruti's and Van's blessings. Van's was just like the sword in his hand. Ruti's was the true version, modeled after the soul of the Asura demon who was the first hero, while Van's was a knockoff created by God.

"Yes. The people forgot the love of God. The only thing that could be done to save those sad people was to force them to abandon all the civilization they had developed. God has always loved people. And it is thus even now."

Demis did not feel any regret or compassion for the lives he stole and destroyed.

There was only love, a love that killed in order to save.

Souls were reborn. So to Demis, a person's death was nothing more than the next step in sending a soul to its future physical embodiment... There was no tragedy in it.

"I won't accept that," I growled, gripping my sword tightly. "This world is filled with bloodshed. Countless lives are lost every day."

"Death is not the end," Demis answered gently. "All life merely continues after, swaddled in God's love. The lives you speak of are but transient dreams."

"This moment! Not the next life! Now! Lives here are precious!"

My life in Zoltan with Rit—this life was happy.

Seeing Ruti freed from the Hero and having fun and smiling with Tisse—that was bliss.

In this world, where living in accordance with your blessing was efficient, I chose to exist the way I wanted.

I couldn't accept Demis or anyone else who trivialized Van's will and his life!

"Wait, Red!"

Rit broke in front of me before I could act.

Her healing magic breathed energy back into me and Lavender, who still lay on the ground.

"Don't stop me, Rit! I can't forgive him!"

"I know! But can you win?!"

"But he—!"

"Forgetting yourself in anger isn't like you at all! Danan or Esta might get stronger when they're angry, but that isn't how you fight!"

Rit's words cooled my head just a little bit.

A chance... Do I have a chance?

My opponent was God. The Hero had been raised to level 100.

This enemy was beyond anything imaginable, a being more powerful than Ruti the Hero or Demon Lord Taraxon.

"There's no choice but to trust my fate to the sword," I said.

"Don't stop thinking!"

"The only reason we're even speaking right now is because of Demis's mercy. He's allowing us the time for a final conversation before killing us."

Demis wasn't wary in the slightest. If he could defeat Danan or Esta in an instant, he could kill the likes of us with ease at any moment, too. He was simply waiting for us to work up the resolve to die.

"Please, Red! Don't give up! I'll stall for time! So please don't give up!"

"Stall for time..."

"I will, too."

"Albert..."

"Even if it's just one second more, I will stall with Rit. So please..." Albert glanced at the fallen Esta for a moment and gritted his teeth. "Please defeat Demis."

It was an absurd ask.

But I was calm.

I needed to save my comrades. Everyone lying on the ground had suffered mortal wounds. They would die if left there. Only Esta could save them, but she was among the injured.

Her...or Van, with his Healing Hands.

I'd forgotten something important. I needed to rescue Van from Demis as well. I couldn't afford to fail.

"There's a way," I said. "It's one in a million, but there is a way to win."

"Red!" Rit cried.

"But..."

It would take time. No matter how fast I ran, I would need at least six minutes. Surviving for six minutes against Demis was impossible for Rit and Albert.

"Red, believe in me," Rit said.
"Six minutes! I'll leave it to you!"
"Roger!"
All I can do is run! All I can do is believe in Rit!
The moment I started running, Demis moved.
Can't you just wait for me to come back?!
"Ketu Elemental Storm!" came a little voice.
There was torrent of powerful magic.
Crackling lightning, flame, wind—every sort of destructive energy converged on Demis's body.
With blood running from her body, Lavender hurled all her strength at Demis.
"Lavender!"
"Don't look back!" she shouted.
I ran to the exit.
As I left, a large, slender shadow entered the room.
What now? A clockwork dragon?! And clockwork knights are riding on its back!
I didn't look back, but I could sense the clockwork dragon transforming into its original, geared dragon form to face off against Demis.
Demis was the being who destroyed the ancient humans' civilization. They must have understood that Demis was an enemy in their final moments. Their last orders still survived in their clockwork creations.
Calling this good fortune felt wrong. Demis had brought this on himself. The dying wish of the people he had killed, the final blade of the humans who'd been destroyed, would keep God in check.
I ran desperately, calling upon Lightning Speed and Immunity to Fatigue. Demis had granted me my blessing and skills, but they were mine now. I wouldn't accept any complaints about using them.
"The clockworks!"
The constructs marched down the passage one after another toward Demis.
There were this many left in the ruins?

With the last of their power, the clockworks were challenging the deity who'd destroyed their creators.

The lights in the ruins went out. The facility was dying.

Fortunately, we'd already explored the route back.

I just have to remember the way out!

I reached the gondola. There was no time for a leisurely ride, so I jumped onto the rail and used Acrobatics to run along it. From there, I arrived at our camp and kept going.

Van's delight at learning the sword surfaced in my memory.

Calm down. Focus on what needs to be done.

I set my sights on the lowest floor, the deepest point, past the door that Shisandan had opened.

"There!"

It was the final sword remaining from Ruti and Shisandan's battle. This was the weapon that had caused Ruti's blessing to go berserk. I picked up the Sacred Avenger.

It was heavy, like lead. Only the Hero was meant to use this blade. I stowed it in my item box so that I wouldn't feel the weight.

I had what I came for, so I turned and sprinted back to Rit.

※　　　　　　　※　　　　　　　※

The battle was still ongoing when I burst into the room.

Lavender and Albert were on the ground.

The clockworks had been smashed to tiny pieces.

The monsters in the tanks around the facility had even arrived. Amid the piles of countless monster corpses, a juvenile gem beast was the last one standing, although it was on the verge of joining its kin.

Where's Rit?!

"You made it, Red."

"Rit!"

She was still alive.

Her clothes were covered in blood, but Danan, Yarandrala, and Esta were behind her. She'd carried them to a safe place while fighting.

"I believed in you, Red."

"Are you okay?! Your wounds..."

Her hand stopped me.

"They can wait."

"Okay..."

I pulled the Sacred Avenger from my item box.

"That is the blade given by God, is it not?" Demis sounded almost surprised. "Unfortunately, that sword can only be used by the Hero."

"That's not quite true, is it?"

Next, I pulled out the wild elf medicine.

"Poison that rejects God's love," Demis declared.

"Poison that rejects god's love," huh? Sounds like just what the doctor ordered for a situation like this!

I gulped down the medicine. It had a horrible taste.

"You said this sacred blade can only be used by the Hero? That doesn't make any sense. The first hero was an Asura demon who didn't have a blessing," I said.

"Shrewd..."

This sword was a sacred blade that the Hero alone could wield. But it had been given to a creature without a Divine Blessing.

There was one answer that solved that paradox. The Hero blessing wasn't the key to drawing out the weapon's power. Rather, the Sacred Avenger rejected every blessing other than the Hero.

Shisandan had been able to wield it not because he was an Asura demon like the first hero, but because he didn't have a Divine Blessing.

I drank vial after vial of the wild elf elixir. I could feel my skills and blessing growing weaker.

"Sad. God's love can no longer reach you. But God loves you even so."

Demis moved toward me.

Please answer me.

Sacred sword. First hero.

I am no hero.
But please, even if only for a moment, lend me strength.
To save my friends who have fallen.
And also...
"Lend me the strength to save the boy who will someday be a hero!"
I gripped the sword with both hands.

"Very well," spoke a voice in my mind. "The hero is nothing so grand as that. If you wish to save someone other than yourself from the bottom of your heart, that is qualification enough."

You're...

"Just a fragment of a meaningless soul lingering in this sacred blade. I caused you all terrible trouble before...so I shall give you everything I have. Get ready!"

Demis raised his sword.

I saw the movement, the divine speed that even Danan had failed to react to. I saw it clearly.

I moved in sync with the blade.

Defense, and then victory from an instantaneous counterattack.

I saw the ideal form of swordsmanship.

But that will kill Van!

"Believe in the hero's power."

There was a split-second clash. Holy blades crossed.

Power flowed into me through the Sacred Avenger, raising my physical abilities and reaction speed to Demis's level, possibly even higher.

And I wouldn't lose in an even battle of sword techniques.

Demis's sword was knocked to the left as mine came down now that his defense was broken.

"Why do you reject God's love?"

"Because it's a selfish love."

The Sacred Avenger pierced Van's body. I could feel it slicing into him.

But there was no blood... Only Demis's essence was cut.

It was ironic.

This blade was the only weapon in the world made by God; it was the sole armament with that same divine status. That allowed it to reach the hand of God that had touched Van.

"Unfortunate."

Van's body slumped like a puppet whose strings had been cut. I could feel the tremendous power leaving his body.

"Van!"

He rose unsteadily to his feet, as if responding to my voice.

"I-I'm okay… My memory is hazy, but I know what happened."

"You're back! Quickly! Heal everyone!"

Van was still a little wobbly, but he looked me in the eyes and nodded, heading to Lavender first and then everyone else, restoring them with his Healing Hands.

Somehow, everyone managed to make it through.

* * *

The battle was over.

"Rit…are you okay?" I asked.

"I believed in you. I was sure you'd find a way to win."

"This time…this time, I was about to give up. I would have broken without you."

"Ehehe. My Red's amazing."

Rit's wounds had been mended perfectly. Van's Healing Hands ability really was something. Mastering a skill was for more than show.

"Well done."

The voice rang in my ears again.

I'd accepted it earlier, since I had to focus on defeating Demis, but… was I really speaking with the first hero?

I couldn't really help but feel a bit nervous. This was the most legendary hero of them all.

"No need to clam up. I am but a fragment of an Asura who died long ago. You, though—you did well to stand against Demis."

Because you told me to trust you. The opponent was almighty God himself, yet courage welled up inside me.

Surely, that was the power of a true hero's words.

"As I am now, I don't have any such power. That courage was merely what resided in you."

If you say so, then I have to believe you. I'm honored.

"This sword once tormented your sister. I'm glad I could atone for that."

That wasn't your doing. It was because the Hero blessing grew stronger while holding this sword.

"Indeed. In truth, being a hero has nothing to do with blessings or skills. The Hero blessing's nature was shaped by the way I lived my life."

Why did Demis create that blessing? Why did he intervene with a miracle simply because the Hero decided to live his own way?

"I don't fully understand, either. But apparently, my life fulfilled the goal Demis had in making Divine Blessings."

I see…so that's why he used your soul as the model for a Divine Blessing. Demis wanted to have people live as you did, to re-create a soul like yours, I guess.

"Demis is a god who's not content to reap a ripe harvest. He believes he can make a hero's soul like mine by forcing others to live like me. So instead of reaping the fruit, he buries it in the ground, hoping to produce a new crop."

The first hero's voice grew faint.

"It seems your suppressed blessing is recovering. It has been a long time since I spoke with anyone."

Wait! One more thing! What is New Truth?! What is the blessing that appeared in my sister?

"The power of people, the true demon lord, a part of the greatest strength in this world that I challenged."

The true demon lord?

"Take care but do not fear. The demon lord is a power that everyone possesses. Love can also be born from it. How you use it is up to all of you…"

The first hero's final words were so weak, I could only just barely make them out. However, I felt them as surely as if he'd shouted in my ear.

"Brave hero, live in happiness."
With that, the first hero vanished.

*　　　　　*　　　　　*

"Red, are you all right?"

Rit watched me with obvious worry in her eyes.

Apparently, I'd sat down while talking to the first hero.

"How long was I like this?"

"Hmm? Just a few seconds, I think. I asked because I thought you might be tired."

"I see."

I thought my conversation with the first hero had lasted for a minute. Had it really only been a second or two?

The sword in my hands felt terribly heavy.

"He said my blessing has returned, but…my skills still feel weakened."

The effects of the wild elf medicine yet remained.

I'd downed six doses. Typically, you weren't supposed to take more than one.

Will I be okay?

"R-Red, your face looks really pale," Rit said.

"I don't actually know what happens after taking a bunch of that medicine…"

"What? Huh?!"

"There wasn't any other way, so I just…"

"Your blessing reacts to it like a poison, right?! I'll cast Cure Poison!"

Rit immediately conjured a seal and summoned spirits to neutralize the poison.

Hmm, it sort of feels a little better, but also not really.

"It isn't getting better…!" Rit exclaimed.

"I think the toxin of the elixir is gone now, but I guess spells can't heal a blessing disorder. At least we know this isn't some unexpected side effect from the medicine's ingredients. Thank you, Rit."

"Urgh."

Rit looked worried.

"Let me help, too."

"Van."

After healing everyone else, Van approached me and activated Healing Hands.

The trouble with my blessing remained, but my exhausted body did feel much improved.

With my blessing enfeebled, my skills became weaker, so all that fighting put more strain on my muscles and bones than normal.

Now that the battle was over, true hell awaited me.

"Thanks, Van. My blessing isn't improving, but my body is definitely better."

"I'm sorry…"

"You don't need to apologize. God intervened with a miracle."

Obviously, this wasn't Van's fault.

"Thank you for saving my precious friends. Without your Healing Hands, everyone would have died." I meant that with all my heart.

Van looked unsure how to respond, but after a moment, he nodded slightly.

That was enough.

"You just experienced a true miracle. What will you do now?" I said.

"I…will stick to my plan. I still don't know what sort of hero I want to be."

"I see."

"This adventure changed my life as dramatically as the miracle that gave me the Hero blessing… Thank you, Red."

Van remained hesitant, but that uncertainty didn't seem to trouble him the way it used to. His doubts represented possibility.

This was as far as we would journey together… I didn't know what sort of hero he would become. However, he would undoubtedly find a life of no regret.

And that made me happy.

Chapter 4

The End of an Adventure and a Day Off

"Good morning."

I awoke to a voice. My eyelids were heavy, and it felt like my body remained asleep.

"Big Brother."

Ruti's red eyes hovered over my face.

"Good morning, Ruti."

"Good morning…" Ruti looked at me and nodded. "Tisse will make breakfast today, so you can take it easy."

"Hngh. No, I can make breakfast like I always do…"

"You're really exhausted. You have to rest today," Ruti declared. She wasn't going to budge on this.

"Okay, I understand… Can I at least help a little?"

"No."

With nothing else to do, I looked at the ceiling while lying in bed.

There was nothing of particular interest up there.

"Phew…"

The drowsiness hit me instantly.

Normally, this would have been unacceptable. I'd trained myself to wake instantly at the first sound of an enemy's footsteps, no matter the environment.

Yet here I was…bedridden and about to pass out again from overexertion.

"So this is what it's like without any kind of endurance-modifying skill."

I was the Guide. I was born with a blessing level of 31, and I started taking skills the moment I was aware of that. A life without skills was completely new to me.

"Ruti told me to rest, so maybe I should just sleep a little more."

I gave in to the drowsiness and closed my eyes.

As I dozed off, I thought about the recent adventure.

After the battle with Demis was over, we returned to camp, and I told everyone what I'd learned. Then we went through the spoils we'd taken from the facility.

Speaking with the first hero had been a shock, but it hadn't changed all that much. He'd validated our chosen way of life, so there was no reason to question ourselves.

Before we left the ruins the next day, I returned the Sacred Avenger to its original resting place. Despite being the Hero's sword, it was quite dangerous for the Hero to wield. Van would carry one of the holy blades made by ancient humans instead. It was a mighty sword that would undoubtedly delight Cardinal Ljubo.

With Ruti's Holy Demon Slayer broken, Van's weapon was now the strongest in the world. It would lead him to victory against the demon lord's army.

We decided not to tell Ljubo what happened in the ruins. What we learned there was enough to turn the world on its head. We told him that it'd been an adventure to find equipment the ancient elves left for the Hero. Esta and Van did an excellent job of convincing him.

That brought the whole incident to a nice, neat conclusion.

A lot happened, but it was a good adventure.

Firewood crackled from some other room.

There was a mouthwatering scent.

A chikuwa stew for breakfast?

"Redddd!"

"Gyah?!"

I'd been comfortably enjoying sleeping in when something small forcefully kicked my nose. I held it and rolled out of bed from the sudden shock.

"Oh? I didn't think you would take that much damage."

"Lavender...my skills aren't working, so I'm weaker."

"Hmph. It was pretty funny. Can I do it again?"

"Absolutely not!"

Lavender had come flying in and kicked me. What was this all about?

"Well, it's a short errand, so I'll leave soon."

"A short errand?"

Apparently, she had some business with me. Here I was thinking she'd kicked me for no reason.

"You saved Van from Demis... Thank you," the fairy mumbled.

"Oh? Never thought I'd hear that from you."

Were pigs going to fly next?

"Here, this is for you. As thanks for saving Van."

Lavender threw a stone the size of a fingernail at me.

"Oh!" I frantically moved to catch it. My reflexes were dull, and I almost missed. Opening my fingers, I saw a jewel resting on my palm.

"Is this...a blue sapphire?!"

"Shh! Not so loud!"

Lavender raced to cover my mouth.

I nodded.

"You understand? Good. If Rit heard you, it would ruin the proposal she's been waiting for."

"How did you—?"

"I've said it before. With a word, I can get gold or jewels or whatever else I want."

She had no qualms about leaning on her archfay privilege.

People who had to serve high-ranking types like her usually had it rough. As a former knight, my stomach ached a bit.

However, the best thing to do was be glad for the gift.

A blue sapphire really did suit Rit's sky-colored eyes.

I'd journeyed to the Wall at the End of the World and fought a gem beast to get a blue sapphire for Rit's ring. Ultimately, the monster ate all the jewels, though, so I was never able to get one.

"I finally got my hands on a blue sapphire."

The time had finally come.

* * *

Wide-awake now, I slipped the jewel into an interior pocket of my shirt.

Clothes for adventurers were always made with such pockets, which thieves couldn't reach. Removing objects from them was difficult, but they were perfect for storing something precious you received from a client or an item you wanted to keep on you at all times.

"Good morning, Red!" Rit greeted me cheerfully.

"Good morning, Rit."

"Hmm? You must still be tired. You seem a little different from usual."

"Ha-ha, it's probably just because my blessing is weakened. Though, I am pretty tired, too."

The biggest reason was the thing in my pocket…

I had to make sure she didn't find out.

Her knowing wouldn't really be a problem. I'd already told her my plan when we went out hunting for gems before…but I still wanted this to be a surprise.

"Ah, good morning, Red."

"Good morning, Tisse, Mister Crawly Wawly."

The spider on Tisse's head raised his right foreleg in greeting.

"We were just setting out breakfast," Tisse said.

"I'm here, too." Ruti waved to me while holding plates from behind Tisse.

So cute.

"Today, I made an *oden*-style stew using Oparara's *chikuwa*, along with some *chikuwa* bread," Tisse declared.

I regarded the statement dubiously. "*Chikuwa* bread?"

"It's delicious," Tisse replied, brimming with confidence.

She and Mister Crawly Wawly had both taken the Cooking skill. And they had talked with Oparara a lot. The food they made was sure to be tasty.

I couldn't help chuckling a bit at how the bread looked with the *chikuwa* sticking out of it.

Tisse didn't show it much, but she had a sense of humor. This kind of food suited her well.

*　　　　　*　　　　　*

""Thank you for the meal.""

After eating, everyone helped clean up the dishes.

I wanted to pitch in, but I was told to rest again. Thus, I remained sitting in my chair and leisurely sipped tea.

It had been a delicious breakfast.

"This is relaxing…"

I never would have expected Demis himself to show up. Thinking back, it was incredible that we managed to make it out alive. Paired with the fight against Van, that was two battles that were bad for my heart paired back-to-back.

But that was over now!

With Veronia aiding humanity and Van the Hero joining the fight with the *Vendidad*, the idea of driving the demon lord's army from the continent seemed very plausible.

Van was sure to leave his mark in history as a grand hero. My job as the Guide was done.

"Now then, I need to refill the medicine stocks that were depleted while we were away," I said.

"You can do that tomorrow!" Rit shouted as she returned from putting away the dishes. "There are other apothecaries in Zoltan, so you don't have to push yourself!"

"Well, there's no sickness going around, and no monster swarms have popped up recently, so I guess you're right."

Preparing medicine would be difficult without skills.

I'd compensated for a lack of dexterity with a wealth of practical skills, and now that they were weakened, I wasn't much good at work.

"Yeah, it's probably better if I just rest," I said with resignation.

"Right." Rit beamed.

"That's enough," Ruti agreed. "You worked really, really hard, Big Brother. You should take a day to recover."

"Ruti, Tisse, the breakfast was great," I praised.

"I'm glad you liked it. *Chikuwa* truly is magnificent." Tisse's relatively expressionless face looked proud.

How was it that she ended up loving *chikuwa* so much? *Oden* was eastern cuisine and not popular enough to have spread across the continent. Perhaps a grand adventure had led her to discover *oden*.

"I'll watch the shop. These past few days, I've gotten good enough to be dubbed the shop's poster girl," Ruti said.

I cocked an eyebrow. "Oh?"

"Leave it to me."

Ruti was on fire. What happened while we were at the ruins?

I was a little sad that I hadn't been here to see her growth.

"Wait a second, Ruti! It's Red & Rit's Apothecary, so I'm the poster girl!" Rit protested.

Ruti just shook her head at the complaint.

"You're more like the lady of the house than a poster girl."

"...Who said that?"

"Gonz."

"Gonz, huh?" Rit was smiling, but she looked furious.

Farewell, Gonz. It was nice knowing you.

"I feel bad that you're both working while I do nothing." This was possibly the first day I'd taken a day off alone since Rit moved in.

What should I do?

As I pondered absentmindedly, Mister Crawly Wawly hopped on my shoulder.

"Hmm? What is it?"

He spun his front legs with a rousing look on his face.

"Mister Crawly Wawly says he'll guard you if you're going out," Tisse translated.

He's worried about me because I'm weakened?

Taking a day off with Mister Crawly Wawly didn't sound too bad.

"All right, Mister Crawly Wawly, I'm counting on you."

His body swayed as though to reply, "Leave it to me."

The store opened, and Mister Crawly Wawly and I headed out together.

I'd been down underground for a few days, and it felt like summer had arrived while I was away.

I could already hear the bees buzzing as I strolled through the neighborhood.

"It sure is hot," I muttered.

Mister Crawly Wawly peeked his head out from my clothes and nodded. At first, he rode on my head, but apparently, it was too hot up on my black hair with the summer sun beating down.

Were I in his position, I probably would've hidden, too.

"Big Bro Red!" called a child.

"Hey, Tanta."

It was Gonz's nephew, the half-elf Tanta. He beamed brightly.

"It feels like it's been forever."

"I was out for a few days."

"I went by your store a bunch of times, but you were never there."

"Sorry, sorry. There's been a lot to do lately. But that's all taken care of now."

"Really?"

"Yeah, but don't worry. I'll keep my promise to get a boat so we can have fun."

"It's not just that! There are more things I want to do with you, too!" Tanta grumbled angrily.

Over the course of the Van incident, I'd gone to Sant Durant, a fairy village, and the underground ruins. I'd been away from Zoltan a lot. And this time, I'd left without saying anything, since it was too hard to explain why Red the apothecary was going on an adventure with Van the Hero to explore ancient ruins. That's probably why Tanta was so upset.

"In that case, do you want to play some now?" I suggested.

"Can we? You don't have an errand to run?"

"I'd planned to visit Mogrim, but that can wait until the afternoon. I left Rit to run the shop while I take the day off."

"Ohhh! I thought you never did anything without Ms. Rit." He looked genuinely surprised.

"Do we really spend that much time together?"

"Yes."

"Oh."

There wasn't much I could say when the kid nodded that seriously.

"So what should we do?" Tanta asked.

"What do you want to do?"

"Let's talk about how to renovate your store."

"Oh? Renovations, huh?"

"There are lots of things you should probably change once Ms. Rit has a baby, right?"

"A baby?!"

"What are you getting embarrassed about?" Tanta asked.

"You're talking about having kids."

"Aren't you an adult? You need to stop getting embarrassed and think about what you'll do when you have a kid. A home isn't done once it's built. A home grows along with a family!"

"Right…"

I couldn't argue with that.

Tanta had the look of a proper craftsman. I was ashamed of getting so awkward over this.

"Interior design will be key. You need to put some serious thought into how things will change after you two have a kid!"

"G-got it."

Tanta pulled some paper and wax pens out of his bag and started sketching out the interior of a room.

I was going to have to take this seriously.

I imagined Rit and me there, a small baby in her arms. I'd reach out, and the infant would squeeze my finger.

What a happy future.

Tanta and I talked about renovations for a while.

※　　　　　　※　　　　　　※

Come noon, I was walking down the street looking at the sketch of a children's room that Tanta had given me.

"You think it's pretty good, too, right, Mister Crawly Wawly?"

He poked his head out and looked at the picture, then clapped his forelegs together. Apparently, he liked it.

"You'll babysit once we have a child? Ha-ha, that's reassuring."

I laughed a bit, imagining him waving a rattle to soothe a crying infant. He was swaying some, too, perhaps enjoying himself.

"It really is hot, though…"

The heat was getting worse as the sun rose in the sky.

The sunshine was intense, and there was a swell of warm air rising from the ground.

"Want to grab a drink at the place over there?"

Mister Crawly Wawly nodded.

"Welcome." The waitress greeted us cheerfully when we stepped inside.

A few people from the neighborhood were exhausted and hiding from the heat.

It was a typical Zoltan scene. Somehow, it made me feel hotter.

We took a seat at an empty table.

"What can we do for you?"

"We'll have a beer and a water."

"Would you like any food to go with that?"

"Hmmm...what would you recommend to go with a beer?"

"How do Cataphract-style meatballs sound?"

"Oh? The chef is from the north? Then an order of the meatballs, please."

"Sure thing."

The waitress headed into the kitchen.

The drinks and food were on the table in no time.

I took a bite of the meatballs first.

Hmm, there's a nice kick of garlic to it. It's definitely different from the standard Zoltan recipe.

It was tasty. But more importantly...

"Why is a cold beer so good on a hot day?"

I drained the mug with gusto.

A cold beer at noon on a hot day was just perfection.

Mister Crawly Wawly drank his water with similar enthusiasm.

Despite the heat, it was a peaceful day.

"Whoa! What the—?!"

"Where'd you come from?!"

The outbursts prompted me to look around. I saw that a horse had come through the door. Its hooves clicked against the floor as it approached.

"Are you a friend of Mister Crawly Wawly?" I asked.

Mister Crawly Wawly hopped up and down. The horse whinnied as if in answer.

"It doesn't look like you were just passing by and stopped into say hi."

The horse whinnied again and snorted. It sounded serious, but unfortunately, I couldn't really understand it.

"Mister Crawly Wawly, what's your friend saying?"

He used the water on his plate to draw a map on the table and started explaining. This was one clever spider.

"Hmm, so his mate disappeared, and the owner is unreliable, so he went looking for help to find her."

Mister Crawly Wawly waved his forelegs happily. Perhaps he was glad to have conveyed the message to me successfully.

A missing partner, huh…

"What will you do?"

Mister Crawly Wawly looked troubled. He'd agreed to guard me, so he couldn't run off to help his friend. Still, a missing mate was a big deal and a race against time.

Horse or not, that wasn't something to ignore.

"Can I go with you?"

Mister Crawly Wawly hopped joyfully.

I gulped down the last of the beer and stood to find this horse's missing mate.

This world was filled with battle, but it was just as full of adventure, too.

* * *

Three hours later.

"That's things settled!"

Mister Crawly Wawly and I toasted with some well water to celebrate a safe resolution.

The story went like this:

First, we investigated the pasture the mare disappeared from. We were able to pin down that the perpetrator was a griffon.

After that, we tracked down the griffon and retrieved the horse. However, the griffon had apparently been searching for a mare to be his mate. Griffons preyed on horses, but occasionally, they fell in love with one.

Then we ended up looking for a mate for the griffon. Also, we defeated the beast hag that caught the griffon and tried to dominate it.

Finally, we found a horse willing to accept the griffon, and everything ended happily ever after.

I was sure a splendid hippogriff child would arrive this time next year.

"Whew, that was a pretty wild day."

Although my blessing was weakened, my fighting style didn't rely on magic or Martial Arts. And Mister Crawly Wawly was there, too, so a small problem like today's wasn't much trouble.

However, this was supposed to be my day off.

In a world filled with adventure, you could stumble onto a quest just by walking down the road. And Zoltan had fewer adventures than most towns.

Also, the client was none other than Mister Crawly Wawly's friend, and the adventure concluded happily, so all's well that ends well.

I'd even walk away with some profit once I sold the feather we got from the griffon. Plus, it would make a fun story to tell.

"Not much tastes better than water after a nice adventure."

It was just simple well water, but it was refreshing and cool, which made it all the better. Beer on a hot day was great, but cold water was probably still the best.

"Do you always have adventures like this?" I asked.

Mister Crawly Wawly raised his right foreleg in response.

I'd imagined him always being with Tisse, but it looked like he acted on his own quite a bit, too.

Thinking back, the animals at the pasture had a lot to say to him.

"One day, I want to hear the stories of some of your adventures."

Mister Crawly Wawly waved both of his forelegs happily.

* * *

As I approached Mogrim's shop…

"Mr. Red!"

…I heard a familiar voice.

"Al! I didn't know you were back in Zoltan!" I exclaimed.

Al's and Albert's old comrades came running over.

"Oh, wow, Mistorm and Godwin, too," I added.

"It's been a while."

"Hey there, apothecary."

Behind Al were Mistorm the retired adventurer and Godwin the thief-turned-merchant who managed a trade route to the Wall at the End of the World.

"You look like you're doin' well, too, Mister Crawly Wawly." Godwin smiled when the spider poked his head from my clothes.

"Why are you in Zoltan, Al?" I asked.

"We had a delivery to make at the Zoltan Adventurers Guild. We can only stay for a little while, but we talked it over and decided to go visit our family and friends. We just finished our business at the guild!"

"Ah, I see."

"I was planning to visit your shop, too. I never thought we'd run into you out here!"

Seeing how glad he looked, I couldn't help but smile as well.

"You should still come by. I'm sure Rit would love to see you," I said.

"Of course!"

Al had grown bigger and stronger. The time he'd spent staying at our house felt so long ago.

"I was just telling old stories to some youngsters at the Adventurers Guild," Mistorm said.

"I was there putting in a request to fix up the road when Al and the others found me. They had me surrounded. Things looked pretty rough for me until Master Mistorm stepped in," Godwin explained, embarrassed.

"Right," I replied. "I forgot you were the one who broke in to kidnap Al."

Al and his party had likely planned to interrogate him and find out why he wasn't in prison.

Mistorm started chuckling. "The look on his face was priceless. In the end, we settled things by having Godwin treat everyone to a nice meal."

"Ah, so that explains this odd procession," I remarked.

This world was truly full of surprises.

"Were you busy with something?" Godwin inquired.

"Yeah. As a matter of fact..." I pulled out the blue sapphire from my pocket. "I was going to get a ring made and propose to Rit."

"What?!" Al shouted in surprise.

"You actually found one. Not bad, Red," Mistorm praised.

"So Rit the hero and the apothecary are finally gettin' married," Godwin muttered.

The pair nodded to themselves.

And then everyone smiled.

""Congratulations.""

It really was nice having people celebrate our happiness.

✻   ✻   ✻

Finally, I arrived at Mogrim's shop.

On any other day, I would have been there in no time, but it had taken quite a while today.

"Sorry for dragging you all over, Mister Crawly Wawly."

His body shook, and then he swayed, assuring me that he had fun.

Yeah, it was a pleasant trip.

"Red, eh? Break your sword again?"

"Hey, Mogrim. No, this is about something else." The dwarf blacksmith appeared from the back of the store. "Mink isn't watching the counter," I remarked.

"Her stomach's gotten bigger, so she only watches the shop for half the day now."

"Wow. Time flies."

Mogrim's wife, Mink, was pregnant. It became clear she was with child last winter, and now spring was almost over. Of course she was showing by now.

"If I'm bein' honest," Mogrim began, "I wish she would just rest all day, but apparently, that's not great for a mother. It's my first kid, so I don't really know about any of that stuff."

"Your first kid, huh? I'm sure there will be a lot of new experiences."

"When I put my ear to her stomach, I can tell the baby's moving..."

Mogrim's gruff, bearded face was a mess. I'm sure he was struggling to contain all his excitement and joy at the idea of his child being born.

I remembered Tanta's sketch that I had tucked into my pocket and imagined a future with a child.

Yeah, it'll be great. And the first step...

"Mogrim, I'm here with an important request."

"Hmm? If not your sword, then what? Come to buy a kitchen knife or something?"

"Actually..." I set the blue sapphire on the counter.

"This is—!"

"Yeah. I want you to make an engagement ring!" Mogrim wrapped me in a massive hug. "Wh-whoa."

"Well done, lad! I always regretted not bein' able to make a ring for the two of you!"

I gently tried to extract myself, but his thick arms would not yield.

Ultimately, I surrendered to the embrace.

Mister Crawly Wawly moved to the top of Mogrim's head and danced with joy.

"Three days?!"

Mister Crawly Wawly jumped a little in shock. My outburst had startled him.

"You can make a ring in three days?!"

"Aye. Matter o' fact, I already made the ring's base."

"I never put in an order, though..."

"You're the sort of man who follows through when you say you'll do something. Whether it was a blue sapphire or a diamond, I knew

Chapter 4: The End of an Adventure and a Day Off

you'd get the stone you were after eventually. I figured it would be good to prepare in my free time."

Mogrim examined the gem through a small loupe. "Hmm."

"How is it?"

"This here's a great gem. Easily the best of all the blue sapphires I've ever seen." Mogrim nodded with evident admiration. "I can make the ultimate engagement ring with this!"

"Ohhhh."

Mogrim was fired up.

Lavender had apparently acquired a spectacular gemstone.

I needed to thank her the next time I saw her.

"All right, with that settled, we need to pick out the design! You had dinner yet, Red?"

"No, not yet."

"Then you're eating here tonight! The store's closed for the day!"

Mogrim hurried outside with heavy footsteps and hung the CLOSED sign out on the door.

"Oy, Mogrim! I wanted to check out a secondhand spear!"

"No one asked you! Come back tomorrow—we're closed today!"

"But—"

Mister Crawly Wawly swayed as though shaking his head at the scene.

✳   ✳   ✳

It was night by the time I headed back to the shop.

A shady man approached me as I walked toward home.

"Hey, you look pretty skilled. Interested in making some money?"

"No, I've got enough adventure in my life."

"Wait, you can get rich gathering the horns of fire almiraj—"

Ignored.

The light from my house came into view.

"*Phew*, we finally made it back. Thanks for all your work, Mister Crawly Wawly."

He raised his right foreleg snappily. Then he tapped his head and looked at me.

"Hmm? Did I have a fun day off? Yeah, it was a great time."

It truly was.

Home got closer with every step.

"Red!"

"Big Brother."

Rit and Ruti were sitting on the bench out in front of the store.

"Were you waiting for me?" I asked.

Rit nodded. "The moon is lovely tonight, so we thought it might be nice to wait outside."

"We have snacks, too." Ruti showed me a plate filled with nice, round cookies.

"Those look tasty."

"Did you eat already?" Rit inquired.

"Yeah, I had dinner over at Mogrim's place."

"Oh? How is Mink doing?"

"Her stomach has gotten quite a bit bigger. Mogrim is trying to keep her from working in the shop too much."

"Heh-heh. I bet he'll be a good father," Rit said.

I brushed off the dirt on my clothes and joined her and Ruti.

"Isn't this bench a little tight for three people?" I asked.

Rit shook her head. "No, this is good. The big, luxurious chairs in the palace were okay, but it's nice being close enough to touch shoulders, too."

"Really?"

I had sat down in the middle, in the space Rit and Ruti had left between them. Rit was to my right, and Ruti to my left. We snacked on sweets while our shoulders touched. The ample amount of egg used in the cookies made them rich and tasty.

Mister Crawly Wawly leaped down to the ground and raised his right foreleg. He was surely off to see Tisse inside.

"Thanks for today. You should tell her what happened," I said.

He nodded as though to reply, "Of course," then hurried into the house.

"How is your blessing, Big Brother?"

"My skill level has come back a bit. At this rate, I should be back to normal in around a week."

"Good."

"Once I recover, what should I spend my new skill point on? It's my first level up since coming to Zoltan. Maybe I should invest it in a common skill I've never considered before."

"Like what?" Rit asked.

"Hmm, what indeed…?"

There were a lot of common skills, but…

"Steering might be a good one. I kind of want to try flying the airship."

"Ohh! I've gone to check where it's kept, but I haven't seen it in action."

"It'd be nice to ride it sometime," I agreed. Rit nodded, and I did the same.

"I entrusted the airship to Tisse, so you can ask her about it later. If you do go flying, I want to come," Ruti said.

"Sounds like fun." I'd suggested Steering as a bit of a joke, but it was beginning to sound like a good choice. "Or maybe Drawing?"

"Drawing?" Rit smiled. "That'd be lovely!"

The Drawing skill allowed you to sketch out anything you saw or imagined.

It wasn't particularly useful for combat or on trips. It could be handy for creating a map, but you needed precise scale measurements for maps. The Survival skill or something similar was better for that.

Thus, I'd never considered the Drawing skill while I was a knight.

"What prompted you to think of Drawing?" Rit asked.

"Some stuff happened today that involved pictures is all."

I showed her and Ruti the picture that Tanta had made for me. He hadn't connected with his blessing yet; he'd done it without the help of a skill. It was the work of a child, but it was still good enough to convey an idea for our house.

I also had the plans Mogrim made while we talked about the ring's design, but that could wait for another three days.

"Tanta drew this for me. It's a design sketch for future renovations."

"This is…a child's room," Rit whispered.

"Yeah, it looks nice, right?"

Rit smiled. "Ehehe. It's lovely."

"I'm curious what sort of things you did on your day off, Big Brother," Ruti commented while looking at the drawing.

"I ran into Tanta in the morning. He drew this while we played around until about noon… Actually, you haven't heard about everything that happened in the ancient elf ruins yet, right? I should go over everything."

"Mm. I would like that."

"It might be a little long…but it's not too warm to sit outside and chat for a while."

I told Ruti the story of our adventure.

A lot of things happened.

We learned the truth about the Hero Administration Bureau and that the ancient elves were actually humans. We saw Van's growth and Demis's miracle that overwrote it all.

"Demis?!" Ruti froze up in shock at that part. I understood why. God had literally intervened during our adventure. "I really should have gone with you. That sounds dangerous."

"It was. I seriously thought it was over this time," I replied.

"I lost hope, too, but seeing you lose your cool made me feel like I had to keep my head about me…," Rit said.

"And that's what saved me."

Without Rit, I would've charged at Demis in rage and despair. He was so overwhelmingly powerful that I'd completely given up hope.

"I want to give Demis a good punch," Ruti growled, shaking her fist. To her, Demis was the mastermind who'd forced the Hero blessing on her and made a giant mess of her life. It was only natural that she wanted to give God a beating. "But as long as you're safe, Big Brother, then it's all right."

"Are you okay, Ruti?" I asked. "With everything we learned about the Hero, I mean."

Van had been badly shaken by how previous bearers of the Divine Blessing of the Hero lived. However, Ruti just shook her head.

"I'm not the Hero anymore."

"Right."

She'd already turned the page on that story. I'd been a little worried about telling her, but she'd truly overcome the bonds of her blessing.

After that, I recounted what transpired after the battle and what happened today. That included the run-in with Tanta, the adventure with Mister Crawly Wawly, reuniting with Al and Mistorm, having dinner at Mogrim's place, and Mink talking about her future child.

And I also talked about how happy I was to spend time with everyone.

"A lot happened even though you took the day off," Rit commented.

"Yeah, but it was a fun day. This is my slow life."

This world was full of adventure and fighting. That was as true here in the small backwater of Zoltan as anywhere else. Even heroes couldn't change this world. But I was free in my heart. No matter what the world was like, I was determined to be happy.

And we were.

Epilogue
The Ring to Mark a Happy Ending

Evening, three days later.

"I have the ring, right?"

I touched the little box in my pocket, just to make sure.

How many times did that make? I couldn't help grimacing internally a little. I didn't have the Hero blessing, so I got scared.

I was sitting on the bench out in front of the shop for Rit to come back.

It's the opposite of last time.

"Ah, Red! Were you waiting?"

"Yeah. Welcome home, Rit."

"Ehehe. I'm back!"

Rit hugged me and gave me a light kiss on the cheek.

My heart skipped a beat at the feeling of her soft lips.

"You said you'd start making dinner again today, but are you sure you're well enough? You can keep resting if you like," Rit said.

"No, my Cooking skill is back now. And I like cooking for you."

"Ehehe. In that case, I'll go get changed!" Rit headed inside.

"Oh, all right…"

I touched the box in my pocket.

I couldn't give it to her…

* * *

There was a clinking sound in the kitchen.

I washed a cup with soap and water and handed it to Rit. She took it, wiped it dry with a dish towel, and set it on the shelf.

"There, done," I said.

"Good work." After putting the last cup away, Rit raised her hand, and I gave her a high five. "Yay." We'd only cleaned the dishes together, yet Rit smiled as though we'd finished a big job.

Whenever we did something together, we always ended up high-fiving, shaking hands, or hugging. Well, not when other people were around. Or at least, I don't think so.

Maybe a little bit…

"All right, I'll go get the bath ready," Rit said.

"Thanks."

I went back to the living room and wiped down the table. I carefully wrung out the towel I'd been using to dry.

With that done, I waited around while Rit prepared the bath.

"Hmmm."

I couldn't decide when to give her the ring.

"I'm getting nervous. Maybe I should wait for tomorrow."

I thought to procrastinate, but I quickly shook my head and banished that timid idea.

"Didn't the captain teach me that it wasn't good to draw things out? Once you've decided on something, you should do it without hesitation. Decisiveness makes for an invincible blade."

Of course, that advice was for tactics and swordsmanship. The captain probably hadn't imagined his words could apply to a situation like this.

Recalling them was nostalgic, though. When I first joined the knights and fought using only the power from the level boost that came with my blessing, he taught me the importance of swordsmanship.

"*That's not swordsmanship, Giddo.*" He always said things like that during training, teaching me not to rely too much on my divine blessing.

Epilogue: The Ring to Mark a Happy Ending

"Listen here, Giddo. Blessings are absolutely the source of our strength. But a blessing can't make decisions for you. We have to decide for ourselves what's right."

Blessings couldn't make decisions. People often forgot that fundamental fact. Impulses compelled everyone to obey, giving pain when we resisted and joy when we acquiesced. The church taught that Demis would not blame people for mistakes or crimes that came from them living as their Divine Blessings demanded.

Seven years ago, a ferocious man with a Bandit blessing known as the king of the mountains was executed. It was unknown how many people he'd killed or how much he'd stolen, but the church and most of the townspeople respected him for fulfilling the role set by his blessing. He spent his final days in prison with little restraint. When the date of his execution arrived, many people came to see, and when he trembled from fear of death, the audience cheered him on.

He died to a massive round of applause.

"It always felt weird."

I'd been involved in the battle that ended in his capture. He wasn't really any sort of chivalrous thief. He possessed the sort of charisma that drew people to him, and he was apparently good at looking after his followers, but I couldn't feel any sympathy for him while knowing how many he killed for personal gain.

"The bath is ready!" Rit called out.

Ugh, I was completely lost in thought.

I still hadn't decided on the crucial moment when I'd give her the ring.

I guess I'll think about it in the bath...

✻   ✻   ✻

Rit and I entered the bath together.

She leaned her back against my chest and relaxed comfortably. From behind, I could see the back of her neck and her breasts bobbing in the water. It was a lot to take in, and it made me a little bashful.

We had been out on an adventure for almost a week. It had been a while since we'd bathed together.

"Today was nice," Rit said. A drop of water on the ceiling fell into the bath with a *drip*. "A big adventure was a fun change of pace, but this sort of carefree life with you really is the best."

"When I came to Zoltan, I thought things would be a bit quieter and more solitary."

"Really? Would you have preferred it that way?"

I hugged her shoulders.

"Of course not."

We both closed our eyes and basked in the warmth of each other's bodies.

"R-Rit." I had to say something. "Wh-when we get out of the bath, I want to give you something. Do you have a moment?"

"Huh? Of course. What is it?"

"It's nothing all that important… No, I guess it is. It's something important to me."

"Something important…"

We both tensed at that.

Calm down. Deep breaths.

* * *

There was a legend associated with the custom of giving an engagement ring.

It was a part of the myth of "The Demon of Winter and the Dragon Knight."

After defeating the demon of winter, the dragon knight saved the princess who'd been trapped in a castle of ice. However, the demon's curse kept her frozen through to the heart.

The dragon knight fell in love with the beautiful princess at first sight and grieved that she was frozen. He took a band from his ring finger, put it on the princess's chest, and let a drop of his blood fall through it.

The knight's hot blood passed through the princess's skin and warmed her frozen heart. Life returned to the princess, and she slowly opened her eyes. Then the two shared a kiss.

Afterward, the dragon knight married the princess and returned to her homeland, where he became king.

That was the gist of the story.

That's how the custom of giving an engagement ring began on Avalon. Wearing it on the ring finger similarly originated from that myth.

The story was an obvious metaphor—a drop of blood through a woman's ring…

While waiting for Rit to get changed after getting out of the bath, I picked up the little box and fretted that I should have waited for a better day. Perhaps I could have given it to her at some nice restaurant. I worried that she might not like it—that she would be disappointed.

✻   ✻   ✻

"I-I'm changed." Rit stepped out in her usual attire instead of her nightgown. "S-sorry, but I like this outfit. Fighting with you as a comrade in Loggervia, living together as partners… I can't really express it well, but every day with you is more precious to me than some special event. So I thought this outfit was better… Is that okay? Should I change into something prettier?"

"No, I love you in those clothes, too."

We both blushed.

Rit tried to cover her mouth with the bandana around her neck, but she stopped and clenched her fist while looking straight at me.

"What did you want to give me?"

Looking straight into her sky-blue eyes, I felt the ring box in my right hand one more time. I recalled when I met her in Loggervia.

"Loggervia doesn't need some outsider hero!"

That was what she said the first time we met.

She was hostile, but since we were fighting the same enemy, she tried to destroy our credibility by achieving things before we could rather than interfere with us directly.

Rit thought that would change her father's mind about accepting help from the Hero's party and giving us command of the army.

＊　　　＊　　　＊

In the capital of Loggervia, I took out the map from the duke, unfolded it across the desk, and started writing notes about problems to be resolved.

"There are two occupied villages. The demon lord's main force is deployed to the south. There are divisions of orc hussars to the west and east. The supply of lumber from the mountain villages has decreased for some reason. In the newly cleared land to the north, there have been attacks by a monster described as a drake. No request for aid has been sent to the neighboring Duchy of Sunland."

Looking at how the demon lord's forces were deployed, it was clear their end goal was to encircle and lay siege to Loggervia Castle. They attacked villages to cut supply lines and wear down Loggervia's army.

That much was evident by how the demon soldiers didn't engage directly, preferring to send in orc hussars almost exclusively.

"That division of Asura demons concerns me."

Asura demons were fearless elites who made the soldiers of Avalonia shake in their boots. As infantry, their marching speed was extraordinarily fast. Even the most difficult of roads were no problem for them.

In particular, they were skilled at attacks from rivers, striking settlements from little boats. By the time an army gathered to repel them, they would flee to deeper water where they couldn't be pursued.

Settlements were typically formed near bodies of water. People required water to live, and it was essential to agriculture. Transport by river was also an efficient means to conduct trade.

Any map would show lines of towns and villages set along rivers.

"An Asura demon commands the forces invading Loggervia, making this situation all the more perilous. We'll need to prepare for attacks from the water."

With command of Loggervia's forces, it would be a lot easier to deal with that.

"We'll need to make a show of our strength to get the local nobles to accept us, though. Thus, our first step should be to attack the orc hussars and liberate the occupied villages to the east and west."

The door to the room flew open.

"It must be rough holed up in a room when it's so bright outside!"

"Oh, it's just you."

I removed my hand from the hilt of the sword at my hip. Rit eyed me suspiciously.

"Why do you carry a sword inside?" she asked.

"Self-defense. I'd appreciate it if you would knock next time."

"Self-defense for what? This is Loggervia; who do you think is going to attack you?"

I shrugged without answering.

There was no need to tell her that after all the time I'd spent fighting, I couldn't relax without a sword at arm's reach.

"What did you come here for?" I questioned.

"Because I heard something." Rit approached me briskly, smirking. I was lost in her pretty blue eyes for a moment. "The plan to grant you command of our soldiers was put on hold, right?"

"Thanks to a certain someone."

"Thanks for the compliments!" Apparently, she was here to rub it in. "Now you guys can leave to go save some other country."

"Unfortunately, it's not that simple."

Rit's expression darkened, and she grabbed my shoulder when I returned my attention to the map.

"There's plenty of other countries that will gladly accept the Hero. Just go fight there. There's wealth and fame out there, too. You don't have to focus on Loggervia."

"If Loggervia falls, the entire northern front lines will collapse."

"I understand that much. That's why we'll protect it ourselves."

"Protecting it isn't enough. We'll gladly leave once our job is done."

Rit was at a loss for words, and for a moment, her gaze wavered. However, she quickly righted herself and exhaled.

"Fine. I'll accept that you are fighting to help defeat the demon lord's army."

"Thank you."

"So why are you staring at a map in here all alone?"

"I'm analyzing everything we know first so we can discuss what to do as a party."

"Huh? You have a Sage in your party, right? Isn't that his job?"

"Hmm… Well, maybe for some, it is."

Rit's expression softened for the first time when she saw my awkward smile. Perhaps she'd deduced why I was doing this.

"You must have it rough," she remarked.

"I appreciate the sympathy."

Rit's attention turned to the map.

"You've gathered a lot of information so quickly."

"There's not much point trying to set a course without adequate knowledge."

After looking for a while, Rit picked up the pen on the desk and added a note to the map. "There's a lodge here where merchants stay when going to sell supplies."

"A key infrastructure point, huh?"

"And it's not on the map, but there are soldiers there, too. If they're called upon, it could be an advantageous position."

"Hmm, and if the line is drawn here, it will be easier to maintain a defensive."

"What's this note about holding the east?"

"Protecting the surrounding rivers will be significantly more difficult if we lose that area."

"...True. I'll let the army know. I trust you have no complaints?"

"Of course not. But if it looks like the demon lord's main forces are moving in, it would be better to surrender the point and pull back to this area."

"I agree. That spot isn't suited to a defensive fight."

"Our enemy's main forces are still deployed to the south, so it will most likely be a while before they make it that far. The harvest should be rushed as much as possible so that village can be evacuated to this town, along with all the supplies."

"That settlement can't hold many people, though."

"Then we'll need to make preparations for temporary lodgings. Hey..." At my remark, Rit glanced up from the map and looked me in the eyes. "Why are you helping us?" I asked.

"No matter what I say, you don't intend to leave Loggervia until the defensive ends, right? It seems best to pitch in and get this over with quickly rather than let you hang around longer. I haven't accepted you, though, so don't get the wrong idea."

"I see. Well, I appreciate it... You know..." I couldn't help smirking a bit.

"What?" Rit pursed her lips. Perhaps she thought I was mocking her.

I quickly shook my head. "It's nothing mean! I was just thinking how long it's been since I did this with someone else."

"You really do have it rough."

"So anyway...I guess what I'm saying is...thank you."

"D-don't be stupid! It's not like I'm doing this to help you! I'm doing this for Loggervia!"

Rit pulled the bandana around her neck over her mouth.

Evidently, she had a habit of concealing her expression whenever she smiled or got embarrassed.

I found it really adorable. Usually, she was openly hostile toward me and the rest of the Hero's party. That was the moment when I realized I didn't dislike her.

* * *

Klegsna was a village built near a river crossing and connected to Loggervia by a southern road.

The prosperous farming settlement was home to large pastures of horses and cows.

The cattle raised there were famous and had been enjoyed by dukes of Loggervia and kings of Avalon and Cataphract for generations.

If you ever visited Loggervia, it was best to take the southern road. Travelers plotted their journey to stay the night in Klegsna to enjoy the local beef, even if they couldn't afford the highest-quality stuff.

"Stop it! Those are breeding bulls!"

"Hnnh?"

The orc soldier holding a curved orc-made saber wore a sadistic grin as he looked down at the man clinging to him.

"My father and his father before him and his father before him have reared these animals for generations! You took all the cows already! If you take the bulls, our breed will die out! Everything our forefathers have done will be wasted!"

"What do I care?"

The orc swung his saber without hesitation. The blade bit into the man's back. He screamed in pain before collapsing limply.

"The demons said to take all the food here."

The orc started walking back to the bulls, which were tied in a line. However, a little girl stood in front of the cowering animals with her arms spread wide.

"D-don't take Daddy's bulls!"

Next to her, two boys clutched farming tools, their faces pale.

The orc licked his lips.

"Heh-heh…"

The saber, wet with blood from the children's father, hung loose in the orc's grip.

The girl wanted to run in fear at the sight of her father bleeding on the ground, but she closed her eyes and held back the terror.

She and her brothers would die helplessly, but that didn't make their ends meaningless. They had to fight for the sake of their family. Anything less, and they'd regret it for the rest of their lives.

Sensing the orc raise his saber, the girl's mind was on the verge of going blank. Her clenched teeth grated in her ears.

However, the pain never found her.

* * *

"Ghah?!"

My sword and Rit's stabbed into the gaps in the orc's leather armor. The monster dropped and never moved again.

"Are you all okay?!" Rit rushed over to the children. Meanwhile, I went to the farmer and gave him a cure potion.

"I wish I had something stronger, but I'm low on supplies. I hope you don't mind," I said.

"Ugh…" The blood loss had left the farmer barely conscious, but he would live so long as his wounds closed and he didn't bleed out anymore.

"Are you Rit the hero?!" the girl exclaimed.

"Yes. Sorry for being late. I'm here to save this village."

The kids cheered with tears in their eyes. Rit smiled and embraced the children to reassure them, telling them to hide until the fighting was over.

"Don't worry, I'll finish this before dinner," Rit declared.

The girl's eyes widened. "Really?!"

"Really. Believe in Rit the hero."

"Okay! Is that man one of your friends?"

"Huh?"

Rit looked a little startled when the girl pointed at me.

I grinned, despite myself. "Well, am I?" I asked snarkily.

Rit glared at me, causing the girl to look troubled.

"Y-yes, he is!" Rit said hurriedly. "He's one of my friends. He's really strong, so even if the demon lord's army attacks, we'll be fine!"

"Wow!"

The children looked at me with sparkling eyes. It was all I could do not to laugh.

"Thank you, Ms. Rit's friend!"

Rit seemed a little bit put off.

* * *

"Don't laugh!"

Rit tried to kick me in the back when I started snickering after we left the pasture. Naturally, I didn't let her hit.

"Quit dodging!"

"Why should I?"

I was supposed to be paired with Theodora during the fight to liberate the village.

We planned to wait until the monsters assembled to report to their commander before springing a surprise attack. From there, Ruti and the others would strike, slaying the commander to shatter the orcs' morale and rout them.

Our force didn't even break the double digits, so we couldn't take on an entire army alone. We had to wait for the right moment.

Rit had tagged along because she supposedly wished to see how we fought. Originally, she intended to go with Ruti and the group targeting the commander. However, she couldn't bear to watch the demon lord's forces pillage the town. Thus, Rit and Theodora had switched places, pairing me with the princess.

"Argh! What was I supposed to say?! 'No, he isn't my friend'?! That would just make her worried!"

"True. You really are a thoughtful, reliable friend."

"Grrrr."

While we bantered, we saw four orcs walking around on what seemed to be a patrol.

"Four orcs up ahead."

"I'll take the two on the left."

"Okay, I'll get the right two, then."

The orcs started shouting when they noticed us.

We'd acted quickly to save the kids before, but we delayed our attack this time. A little commotion would help our plan.

"All right, that's probably good enough."

I drew my sword and rushed forward.

"What're you doing here?!" The orcs drew their sabers, one of which blocked my first attack.

"Not bad," I remarked.

The other three immediately tried to cut me down.

"Having trouble already?" Rit came flying in with a shotel in either hand.

Using the weapons' unique curve, she evaded an orc's attempt to parry and cut into him. The orc who had blocked me lost concentration, and I pushed back against his sword and stabbed my blade into his left shoulder.

"Gya!"

"Ugh!"

The two wounded monsters stumbled back, clutching their wounds before falling over. The remaining two stood back-to-back, showing no sign of fear. They looked confident, even after seeing our abilities.

They were likely pretty strong.

""Synchronized Martial Art: Alpha and Omega Wind Blades!"" A storm of slashes erupted all around the orcs.

"Kh?!" For the first time during the fight, Rit looked tense. We both jumped back to avoid the countless blades of wind.

"Now and then, the demon lord's army has some very capable warriors…," I whispered.

I looked down at the scratches on my armor, remnants of attacks my sword had failed to catch. Rit's sleeves were torn up, too. We'd both escaped without any injury, but breaking through to the orcs would be difficult.

"I am Gaderut, which means *fire bird*."

"I am Vijurut, which means *lightning bird*."

""To face the thirteenth hussar's VijuGade means fortune has abandoned you!""

These were likely orc champions, fearless warriors who had survived countless life-and-death battles and reached high blessing levels.

"Synchronized Martial Art...," I muttered.

Such skills boasted increased efficacy when activated by two or more people at the same time. This one triggered when the Martial Arts Alpha Wind Blade and Omega Wind Blade were activated simultaneously.

"It's my first time seeing this one," I remarked.

It was best to finish off powerful opponents like these two swiftly.

I tossed a throwing knife to test the waters, and the wind blades immediately struck it down. Rit tried a Fire Arrow conjured with spirit magic, but it was similarly repelled.

"Projectiles and magic mean nothing before us!"

That didn't sound like a bluff. A heavy-hitting spell from Ares or Theodora might fare better, but Rit's magic would have a tough time.

"Argh!" Rit raised her shotels, ready to charge.

"Wait." I held her back with an arm.

"Huh? When did you—?"

I'd used my Lightning Speed to move next to Rit. The orcs looked shocked for a moment, but they quickly recovered.

"A skill to quicken your movements? Speed is worthless against our technique!"

True, their Martial Art covered every direction, so my Lightning Speed wasn't enough. All the skill did was improve my running. It was powerless against a storm of infinite blades.

Rit glared at me. "You're not going to suggest we flee, are you?"

"Of course not. But we can't afford to let them waste our time."

"So why didn't you let me charge them?"

I put more strength into my grip and looked Rit in the eye.

"Wh-what...?"

"It would be better if we worked together. I'll handle the defense, so you follow behind and focus on offense."

"Work together... I'll admit, you have a point. But..." Rit head-butted me in the forehead. Oww. "...You've got it backward. My two-sword style is better for fending off multiple attacks, and your longsword has more reach. You have two more steps' worth of range. Do you think it's a knight's job to protect women? Don't be stupid!"

Rit met my gaze while pressing her forehead to mine.

She was right.

"Sorry. Will you protect me?" I said.

"Leave it to me."

Rit took the lead, readying both of her shotels with me behind her.

"Both Alpha Wind Blade and Omega Wind Blade only cover about two hundred seventy degrees individually. One compensates for the other's blind spot. However, there's still a low-density spot—head-on. It's one of their openings."

We ran straight at the orcs, ready to dive in. And that's when the monsters grinned.

"This is our technique!"

"We know the weakness full well!"

""That's not enough to break us!""

The two back-to-back orcs turned so that we faced their sides, rotating their storm of attacks to redirect us into the thickest part of the whirlwind.

"Our storm of blades can weather any attack. There's no gap in our teamwork!"

I quickly grabbed Rit's arm and activated Lightning Speed.

"Wh-what?!" she exclaimed.

In the blink of an eye, we moved to the front of one of the orcs again. Thankfully, Rit didn't hesitate, immediately lunging into the storm.

* * *

Ching-ching-ching-ching-ching-ching-ching-ching!!!

Rit's shotels clashed with the enemy's slashes in rapid succession. Her blades deflected the cuts threatening to tear into me. However, by raising her right arm to cover me, she exposed herself. She did well to deflect most of the wind blades with her left hand, but one traced across her thigh.

"Three more steps!" I shouted instead of stopping to worry over her.

One step forward. A second. Blood erupted from Rit's left arm, but she persisted.

The third step.

Rit and I changed places, touching shoulders.

I thrust my sword, piercing one of the orc's armor.

"Nghooooohh!!!" the monster cried.

That's when he grabbed my blade.

"What?!"

He tensed all the muscles of his body, refusing to let me withdraw my sword. The other orc stabbed for my heart.

I held out my left hand; Rit's found it, giving me one of her shotels. I used to slash upward, tearing into the orc hoping to kill me.

That went well, considering I'm not used to wielding shotels.

The first wounded orc's saber stopped just above my neck. Metal screeched against metal. Rit's remaining shotel had caught the attack.

"You didn't try to protect yourself at all. To trust your partner so completely… You're something…"

The orc praised us with a weakened voice. A shotel was buried in the monster's side, tearing through his organs.

"It was a splendid combination." After his partner collapsed, the orc I stabbed pulled my sword from his chest. Blood poured from the wound.

It was a mortal blow.

His red-stained lips twisted, and he collapsed next to his partner.

Rit exhaled deeply and sat on the ground.

"You all right?" I asked.

I handed her a High Cure Potion. She was bleeding from her thigh and the upper part of her left arm.

"Thanks... You're really bad at using a shotel."

"If anything, I deserve some praise for using a weapon I've never held before."

Rit downed the potion in a gulp. She winced, for the magic subjected you to all the pain you would've felt during recovery in one go. However, it passed quickly, and her wounds were closed.

"That's the first time I've fought such powerful orcs," she said.

"They pop up occasionally. The demon lord's army is constantly fighting. A few monsters grow strong from all the war. Orcs battling for the demon lord have higher levels than most," I replied.

"Is it always like this for you guys?"

"Well, it kind of has to be, since we don't have an army. If we don't attempt the impossible, we won't stand a chance against the demon lord's army."

How else were five people supposed to defeat an army of demons that employed sound tactics?

Honestly, it was scary. Facing a dozen orcs or demons with nothing but my sword or armor was terrifying. No matter how many times I did it, I still wanted to run.

Charging through a disciplined line of soldier demons with spears at the ready, weaving through spears that thrust from all angles, the burning heat that came from exceeding my limits as I swung my sword. If I ever lost my weapon, death was guaranteed.

As a result, I'd grown to be anxious without a weapon close by. I couldn't sleep unless there was a sword near my pillow. Falling asleep was easy so long as I had a blade. I could do it just about anywhere. Yet without one, I'd be wide-awake in a city protected by hundreds of soldiers.

"Why the scary face?" Rit asked.

"Ah, sorry. I got lost in thought for a moment."

"When there's more fighting to be done?"

"So says the girl sitting down to rest." I offered a hand, and Rit accepted it, blushing.

"I was just a little winded after defeating powerful opponents."

"There may be more like them," I warned her.

"If there are, then I'll deal with them." Rit's confidence helped me relax a bit. Seeing her face brought me some small relief.

"Will we be working together next time, too?"

"N-no! I'll handle it myself!" Rit took a moment, then stared at her feet as she added, "W-well, against an opponent who's difficult to handle alone, I wouldn't mind working together again. You believed in me. So I trust you enough to fight side by side."

"I see. Thank you for protecting me."

"I'm impressed that you can say that without getting embarrassed," Rit praised.

"You're just really bashful."

"Wh-who are you calling bashful?! Say that again!"

I laughed.

Perhaps that's when I fell in love with Rit. In that moment, I forgot about the battle, my duty, and the weight of the sword at my hip.

Rit's voice pushed them all away. I wanted to talk with her more. I wanted to see more of her.

Her eyes, which reflected the blue skies, her flowing blond hair, her beautiful body, her determined face, that quick shift from anger to laughter, her delicate yet powerful fingers, the healthy thighs beneath her red skirt, and her refusal to rely on others coupled with a determination to stand on her own…

"All of it was so endearing. From that moment on, I always looked forward to seeing you again."

"Red?"

I held out the ring, doing my best to face the feelings building inside me.

I loved her so much. So why didn't I reach out to her in Zoltan? Maybe Ares kicking me out of the party hurt me more than I first realized. I'd feared that Rit would reject me, too, and I couldn't bring myself to say anything.

Despite abandoning the Hero's party without a word, I could never convince myself to leave Zoltan. Similarly, I never gave up my bronze sword, even though I'd set my sights on a slow life free of war.

I was trapped at a crossroads, forever unsure. Yet Rit came to me. She wanted to live with me. And it made me so happy. I grew and became someone who could win any battle against someone who threatened that joy.

Rit was the reason I was still here.

"I've loved you since we met in Loggervia," I confessed.

The emotions finally broke through the dam at my lips. Rit's cheeks reddened. There was no stopping myself now.

"I didn't notice how much I cared initially, but I really do love you."

My speech lacked real structure, but there was nothing for it but to push onward.

I offered the ring in my right hand to Rit.

"Red..."

Rit's eyes shone with tears.

"Would you marry me? No, that's not right. Rit, please marry me. I'm not a hero anymore. I might not be a fitting partner for a princess, but I swear to give you all the happiness I can. I'll make breakfast for you every day."

"Me too... Please marry me, Red. I'm not a princess anymore; I'm just Rit. Still, I swear that I'll love you. Even when we're old and wrinkled, I'll be at your side for the rest of my life."

Rit took the ring from me and put it on her finger.

The blue sapphire matched her eyes perfectly and glittered in the candlelight.

"I'm so happy... It's like a dream."

Tears rolled down her cheeks. I couldn't hold back anymore, either. I held Rit close. Her warmth washed over me.

* * *

Noon, two days later.

""Congratulations!!!""

We were holding a party out on the lawn.

"So you finally popped the question."

"Wimp."

Gonz and Storm both came over to offer their little jabs.

"Tell him how you reacted when you heard, Gonz," Mido said.

"He wept tears of joy, Big Bro," Tanta added.

Gonz's face turned red. "You! What'd you say?!"

"Uh-oh. He's mad!"

"Ah-ha-ha! Run, Tanta!"

Mido picked up Tanta and fled. Tanta laughed heartily as he was carried away.

"You're finally getting married, Rit," Nao said.

"The wedding's still a ways off," Rit answered.

"What are you saying? You said yes, so the wedding should be soon. Men are prone to wavering unless you tie them down quickly."

"Tied down? Was Mido like that?"

"No. He doesn't have the guts for that! He's not much when it comes to muscles, but he's a good, devoted man."

"Sounds nice. I can't wait to have a family like yours."

It seemed like they were having fun.

Mido, Nao, and Tanta were a wonderful family. Would I be able to make one like theirs?

"Red."

"Dr. Newman! You came. I was worried you'd be too busy."

"Of course I did. It's your engagement party. I closed the clinic for the day to celebrate."

"I'm here, too! This salad is really great!" Elenora, the clinic's part-time employee, had also arrived, apparently.

"I'm glad you like it," I said. "I made that salad myself."

"What? You made the food for your own party?"

"Not all of it. But I wanted to do something for everyone revelling with us."

"That's worth a lot of boyfriend points! Rit really does know how to pick them!"

Elenora started eating her salad again. She was really enjoying it. That made the effort of putting it together worthwhile.

"It's a wonderful party."

"Yarandrala."

She walked over to me as Dr. Newman and Elenora stepped away.

"I'm glad you're here," I said.

"I wouldn't miss it. This is your and Rit's engagement party!" Her tone was strong, as though to chide me for being silly.

Oddly enough, that made me happy.

"Congratulations to you, too, Rit!" she added.

"Thank you, Yarandrala," Rit said. The high elf took Rit's hand as she continued, "I found this joy because you gave me that push in the bewitching woods."

Yarandrala smiled. "And I'm glad I did. Thank you for making my friend so happy." She turned her attention back to me.

"Yarandrala."

"Let me hear it from you one more time, Red."

She looked me straight in the eyes.

Memories of our time together surfaced in my mind. We met when I was nine, while I was an apprentice in the Bahamut Knights in the kingdom's capital. She became like an older sister to me while I lived alone and far from my family.

It had been quite a while since then.

"Yarandrala, I'm going to marry Rit."

"Mhm."

"I'm happy. Thank you."

"!!!"

Yarandrala wrapped me in a massive hug.

"Y-Yarandrala?!"

"I was always so worried about you! You always did everything alone! I was afraid you'd work yourself to death, but I couldn't do anything to stop you!"

"I'm sorry for troubling you so much, Big Sis."

People were watching, so I tried to pull away, but I stopped when I heard her sobbing. She was crying… I made a precious friend fret over me for a long time.

"Thank you for finding happiness, Red," she said, voice trembling.

I had some truly great friends.

* * *

Once Yarandrala calmed down, Van and his party approached.

"Congratulations, Red. I don't understand much about marriage, but I can tell you're happy."

"Congratulations, Rit! Mm!!! This is wonderful! I want to marry Van soon, too!"

Lavender was buzzing about joyfully, while Van looked a bit unsure about it all.

Soon, I wouldn't be able to see them anymore. Their business in Zoltan was finished. They'd be leaving in a few days.

"Congratulations, Red."

"Congratulations, sir."

Esta and Albert wished me well together.

"Thank you both," I said.

"To think this day would come. May your paths always be linked in joy." Esta offered a prayer for our happiness, as befit a cleric. "Demis might not accept the prayer, but I wanted to say one for your sake... I've started to believe that is the true nature of faith." Esta smiled.

Ljubo sighed. "I'll pretend I didn't hear that."

"I didn't think Your Eminence would deign to attend."

"I am a cleric. To know my blessing for your union is a rare honor."

The way he said it was a bit...typical of Ljubo. Still, he was trying to show his respect in his own way. He read a wedding blessing for us in a sonorous tone.

That was a cardinal for you. Even the people of Zoltan who hated him stopped eating to listen.

"Thank you very much," I said to him earnestly.

Ljubo cleared his throat. "Also...there is something I should discuss with you."

"Something to discuss?"

"It does not concern me directly... It's more to do with my duty as a cleric. This is hardly the place to discuss it, though. Come see me tomorrow."

"Hmmm."

What could it be?

I didn't sense any malice from Ljubo, so hopefully, it was fine to let it be for today.

Van's party chatted with us a little more before leaving to eat.

Rit came up beside me. "Wow, it's really packed."

We certainly had plenty of guests. There were far more people here than at the apothecary's opening.

Gonz and all our friends from around the neighborhood.

Yarandrala, Danan, and Esta, who'd traveled with me in the Hero's party.

Albert and Van, both of whom I'd crossed blades with in the past.

Al and his group, who happened to be visiting Zoltan by chance.

Mistorm, Mogrim, and Godwin, who'd traveled with me to the Wall at the End of the World.

The regular customers of the store, the doctors—who were especially valued customers—adventurers, and merchants from their respective guilds.

Even Mayor Tornado and the nobles of the Zoltan assembly were in attendance.

And many more...

"Red."

"Hmm? You're..."

It was a young monk from the church.

"You saved me once."

"Right. During the incident with Veronia. You're the young man who got mixed up with those guys from the Thieves Guild."

"Yes, sir! I started practicing with a sword after that. I asked Mogrim to make me one of the same length you wielded." His eyes shone while he spoke.

It was a little uncomfortable.

"I'm still an initiate of the church, but please allow me to honor the man I admire with a prayer for his happy marriage!"

"Thank you, I would love that."

It wasn't as skillful a prayer as Ljubo's, but it was truly heartfelt.

"Congratulations, sir!"

With that, the young monk headed back to the table with the rest of the people from the church.

"It's amazing," Rit remarked. "To think there are so many people who would come to celebrate our happiness."

"Yeah...and I'm not even a knight in Zoltan."

"And I'm not a princess."

Yet still, a whole crowd was here to celebrate.

"It's nice."

"It really is."

We both smiled at each other.

"Big Brother."

"Ruti!"

Ruti, Tisse, and Mister Crawly Wawly were here, too, of course.

"Congratulations, Red."

"Thank you, Tisse."

Mister Crawly Wawly waved his forelegs cheerfully in jubilation.

"Ruti..."

I faced my sister, who looked me straight in the eye.

Before Ares pushed me out of the party, I lived entirely for Ruti. My dream had been to free my sister from the terrible fate of the Hero, so that she might live happily.

"...I'm going to marry Rit."

Her red eyes wavered. Her small lips moved...into a smile.

"You look so happy. And that makes me really glad."

"Thank you. Hearing that means the world to me."

"Congratulations, Big Brother, Rit."

There was a time when I fought to protect that smile. Now Ruti beamed at the thought of my joy. She'd grown so much. What a gift it was to be her brother.

It was a wonderful party.

✱   ✱   ✱

Four days after the party, Van and his party sailed off on the *Vendidad*, departing Zoltan on schedule.

Our raucous days had passed, and we were enjoying a peaceful afternoon at the store.

"Welcome."

"Yo. Sorry for droppin' by unannounced."

A big man in a martial arts outfit entered—Danan.

"Hey, Danan. I haven't seen you since the engagement party."

"Yeah. I had something I wanted to take care of, so I was holed up in my room for a bit."

"Something you wanted to do?"

It was rare for Danan to stay indoors for that long.

"Anyway," he began as he walked over to me. "I'm leaving Zoltan now."

"…That's sudden."

"You don't need to see me off. We can say the good-byes here."

"Why? At least let me take you to the city gate."

Danan laughed. "It's fine. Here works."

Rit frantically rushed over from the back of the store. "You're leaving already?!"

"Yeah! I'm a guy who only knows how to fight!"

"We really should go with you to the gate," Rit said.

"Ah, well…"

Danan scratched his head and then took something out of his pocket.

"I don't really know what sort of gift to give a friend who's getting married…so I decided on something my dad taught me about."

"Is this…a bell?" Danan handed it to me. Ringing it produced a clear, pleasant tone. "Did you make this yourself?"

"Something like that. Kids always end up wandering off, right? These bells produce unique sounds based on their maker's quirks. No other will sound quite like it. So no matter where your kid ends up, as long as you remember the sound of that bell, you'll be able to find them. It's a custom in my homeland. My dad taught me how to make it."

"I never would have guessed."

He'd made a gift for our child.

"That's so sweet. Thank you," Rit said.

"Heh-heh. Anyway, after I've murdered the demon lord, I'll come by to see your kid." Danan smiled as though a little embarrassed. "It would be awkward watching me walk slowly into the distance down the road after giving you that, right? So let's say good-bye here."

"Yeah, all right," I agreed. "Hey, Danan…"

"What?"

"…I'm glad I traveled with you and that I can call you a brother-in-arms."

"Me too! I'm proud to call you and Rit friends!"
He shook my hand and then Rit's. I'd never forget his powerful grip.
"See you, Red, Rit… Be well."
With that, Danan left Zoltan.

✱   ✱   ✱

There were new encounters and farewells.
The heroes left Zoltan, and things returned to the normal, boring, happy daily life.
I had to work on preparing a wedding ceremony. But first, there was one loose end to tie up.
It didn't concern the fate of the world. This was the sort of concern that anyone might experience. Still, it was a big sort of turmoil that could really change the life of the individual going through it and the people close to them.
I thought back to the day I went to talk with Ljubo.

✱   ✱   ✱

I knocked on the door to the inn room where Cardinal Ljubo was staying.
"Your Eminence?" I called.
"Red? Come in."
Ljubo was sipping a glass of red wine and smoking a cigar.
"Importing cigars here is too expensive. Zoltan really should start making its own, don't you think?"
"That's certainly an idea." I shrugged.
He gestured for me to close the door. I did as he indicated and sat in the chair opposite him.
"It's not that big a matter, but…" He set the cigar down. "Well, I'm

grateful to you in my own way. I'm telling you this purely as a show of goodwill."

"I see…"

"It concerns your friend, the boy Tanta."

"Tanta?!"

That was a name I wasn't expecting to hear. Ljubo should've had no connection to him.

"As a Cardinal, I have knowledge and experience with certain blessings."

"Knowledge and experience?"

"The common belief is that determining a blessing before the person in question connects with it is impossible."

"Right. I've heard that even the Appraisal skill doesn't work in that situation."

"Yes, even a skill granted by Demis cannot reveal a blessing before its time. Thus, people believe it is impossible to know until the connection is made."

"Are you telling me that's wrong?" I asked.

"It is wrong when it comes to certain powerful Divine Blessings. And there is a necessity for cardinals of the church to know the signs of those blessings."

"You don't mean…"

Tanta's blessing was…

"If young Tanta would like to be the sort of great person who can fight and win amid the chruch's power struggles, then I will take him under my wing. If not, then Cardinal Marozia would be a good fit. He is relatively *better* among cardinals. I am willing to write young Tanta a letter of introduction."

"Wait a moment, please. Are you saying Tanta's blessing really is…?!"

"Young Tanta has been given the same role as me: Cardinal."

Tanta dreamed of being a carpenter like his uncle—Gonz—and his father, Mido. But there was no guarantee that one's blessing corresponded to their dreams.

"And if neither I nor Cardinal Marozia are satisfactory...then guide him yourself," Ljubo declared.

That went without saying. Tanta was my friend.

I resolved to use all my knowledge and strength to ensure Tanta's blessing did not warp his future.

Afterword

Thank you to everyone who picked up this book!

We've reached Volume 10! My big goal of double digits has finally been achieved!

The story that began with a character who was only strong at the start and was pushed out of the Hero's party once his role was over has become one about seeing off the new Hero.

Red the Guide led a false hero to the path of a true one using what he learned from his slow life, which had nothing to do with his Divine Blessing. Sometimes, some happy endings can only be found on the less direct path.

Red's proposal has been lingering since the fifth volume. With him finally giving Rit a ring, their relationship has passed a crucial juncture. How will things change now that they're engaged? With Van the Hero gone, Ruti will likely play a more active role after lots of work behind the scenes. Even if she accepts the marriage, she still hasn't given up on being her big brother's lover. I hope you'll look forward to the fun messes she might cause.

Now then, let's talk about something that happened between Volumes 9 and 10… I experienced my first-ever traffic accident and had to be sent to the hospital for surgery…

I'll never forget it. Exactly two weeks before the start of the anime, I was walking outside to go get some lunch, and I was hit by a car that ran up onto the sidewalk. I was in the hospital for two months.

Sadly, the anime's first episode aired while I was in a hospital bed after lights out. I was unable to roll over because of my broken leg, so I had to watch it on a small phone screen with a blanket over my head so no one would see the light.

Life is full of surprises, and there's no winning against a car.

Please be careful, everyone. Traffic accidents are no fun at all.

Anyway, while I was incapacitated, the anime adaptation for the series aired from October to December of 2021!

Seeing my story animated, with all the characters moving and talking, really gave me a special kind of joy. Did you all watch as well?

It should be available on streaming and DVD rental, so if you haven't seen it, please check it out!

Ryouta Suzuki's Red is cool, Kanon Takao's Rit is adorable, and Naomi Oozora portrayed Ruti the Hero's conflicted character wonderfully. Taku Yashiro's Ares was perfectly awful, and the performance when he was cornered at the end was superb. Sora Amamiya's Yarandrala gave a great older-sister sort of feeling. The content of the season didn't provide Yarandrala many opportunities to shine, so I'd love for a second season that gives me more chances to see her!

I could go on like this for a while, but there's a limit to how many pages you can put in an afterword, so I'll end this topic here. As the author, I thought it was truly a lovely anime. And if the readers feel the same, then that is all the better.

Masahiro Ikeno's manga adaptation is still ongoing. Tisse's delightful internal reactions are now visible and an absolute must-see. Please check out the manga adaptation! I look forward to each new chapter every month.

And speaking of manga adaptations, the spin-off manga *Banished from the Hero's Party, A Princess Decided to Live a Quiet Life in the Countryside* has started, too.

Mutsuki Higashiooji is drawing it, and it stars Rit as an adventurer in Zoltan after she and Red parted ways in Loggervia. The plan is to tell the story of how she came to be called Rit the hero. Higashiooji is incredibly skilled at drawing sexy, cute women, so I'm really looking forward to this second manga.

Also, a PC game has been released. It's called *Slow Living with Princess*. It features a slightly different scenario from the books, and it involves Ruti suddenly coming to Zoltan alone and living with Red and Rit. There's even a Ruti route for you to pursue.

When I was in middle school, I wrote that my dream was to be a game developer. I never would have guessed that it might come true in a way.

Life really is full of surprises, both good and bad.

Now then, as always, this book could not have been realized without the help of many different people.

My fingers were broken after the accident, a terrifying situation for an author, so I'm grateful to everyone who came to help when I was lying on the sidewalk and couldn't move. I'm also glad for the doctors, nurses, and nurse assistants who worked so hard to help me recover. The physiotherapists and occupational therapists who aided me in regaining the use of my fingers and legs over so many rehab sessions were equally fantastic.

It's because of you all that this book reached the readers. Thank you very much.

Let's meet again in Volume 11!

Zappon
From in front of a poster of Rit, 2022

HAVE YOU BEEN TURNED ON TO LIGHT NOVELS YET?

86—EIGHTY-SIX, VOL. 1–12

In truth, there is no such thing as a bloodless war. Beyond the fortified walls protecting the eighty-five Republic Sectors lies the "nonexistent" Eighty-Sixth Sector. The young men and women of this forsaken land are branded the Eighty-Six and, stripped of their humanity, pilot "unmanned" weapons into battle...

Manga adaptation available now!

WOLF & PARCHMENT, VOL. 1–7

The young man Col dreams of one day joining the holy clergy and departs on a journey from the bathhouse, Spice and Wolf. Winfiel Kingdom's prince has invited him to help correct the sins of the Church. But as his travels begin, Col discovers in his luggage a young girl with a wolf's ears and tail named Myuri, who stowed away for the ride!

Manga adaptation available now!

SOLO LEVELING, VOL. 1–8

E-rank hunter Jinwoo Sung has no money, no talent, and no prospects to speak of—and apparently, no luck, either! When he enters a hidden double dungeon one fateful day, he's abandoned by his party and left to die at the hands of some of the most horrific monsters he's ever encountered.

Comic adaptation available now!

THE SAGA OF TANYA THE EVIL, VOL. 1-12

Reborn as a destitute orphaned girl with nothing to her name but memories of a previous life, Tanya will do whatever it takes to survive, even if it means living life behind the barrel of a gun!

Manga adaptation available now!

SO I'M A SPIDER, SO WHAT?, VOL. 1-16

I used to be a normal high school girl, but in the blink of an eye, I woke up in a place I've never seen before and—and I was reborn as a spider?!

Manga adaptation available now!

OVERLORD, VOL. 1-16

When Momonga logs in one last time just to be there when the servers go dark, something happens—and suddenly, fantasy is reality. A rogues' gallery of fanatically devoted NPCs is ready to obey his every order, but the world Momonga now inhabits is not the one he remembers.

Manga adaptation available now!

VISIT YENPRESS.COM TO CHECK OUT ALL OUR TITLES AND...

GET YOUR YEN ON!

THE JOURNEY CONTINUES IN THE MANGA ADAPTATION OF THE HIT NOVEL SERIES

AVAILABLE NOW

SPICE & WOLF

Spice and Wolf © Isuna Hasekura/Keito Koume/ ASCII MEDIA WORKS